"You don't understand, do you?" Beth cried

"All my life," she went on, "people who did not particularly care for me have been telling me what to do. For the first time ever, I have freedom. You've come to take that away from me."

He looked down at her steadily, his dark eyes thoughtful. "I confess, Elizabeth, that I had not thought of it like that."

He paused, then said quietly, "But do you call this freedom? What are you free to do? Free to become ill when nobody cares? Free to be in danger? I will not offer that kind of freedom to you in Paris. I wish to take care of you."

"But why?" she asked. "I'll only be a nuisance."

In answer, his eyes flashed as he slowly pulled her close....

PATRICIA WILSON used to live in Yorkshire, England, but with her children all grown up, she decided to give up her teaching position there and accompany her husband on an extended trip to Spain. Their travels are providing her with plenty of inspiration for her romance writing.

Books by Patricia Wilson

HARLEQUIN PRESENTS

HARLEQUIN ROMANCE

Don't miss any of our special offers. Write to us at the following address for information on our newest releases.

Harlequin Reader Service
901 Fuhrmann Blvd., P.O. Box 1397, Buffalo, NY 14240
Canadian address: P.O. Box 603,
Fort Erie, Ont. L2A 5X3

PATRICIA WILSON

beloved intruder

Harlequin Books

TORONTO • NEW YORK • LONDON
AMSTERDAM • PARIS • SYDNEY • HAMBURG
STOCKHOLM • ATHENS • TOKYO • MILAN

Harlequin Presents first edition February 1989
ISBN 0-373-11150-9

Original hardcover edition published in 1988
by Mills & Boon Limited

CHAPTER ONE

BETH looked tiredly at the books on the reading-table. Romans in Britain, just about every book they had on the subject, and, having spread them all out over the table, the man had now walked off without even thanking her for bringing them to him. He hadn't even closed the door. She walked over and shut it firmly, wishing that the day would hurry and get itself over.

From the large, plate-glass windows of Collinson's Antique Books she could see the sky was already darkening, making its way towards the short twilight that would herald the end of the day, and it could not come soon enough for her.

She stirred herself into action as Mrs Dennison glanced across at her from the end of the massive shop, as usual sensing the older woman's faint disapproval. Not that Mrs Dennison was ever anything but polite to her; she was impressed by Beth's education, by the name of the school she had attended. It had real snob value.

She was not impressed, however, by the length of Beth's skirts, by the colour of her blouses, nor by the length of her hair which hung down her back like a rope of pure gold, neatly braided but unfashionably long. She was even less impressed by the fact that many nights Beth left the shop on the back of a motorbike, clinging on to Carl Glover's shoulders, her skirts tucked safely around her.

Beth began to sort out the books and take them back to the appropriate shelves. It was a lengthy job, as there were so many and they had to be in very strict order. Many of them were very valuable too, not to be dropped under any circumstances.

'I'm not at all sure that you should have been here today, Elizabeth!' Mrs Dennison caught her as she came from the back of the bookshelves to collect more books. 'You look a little strange. I do hope that you haven't got this bad virus that's going around. If people stayed at home when they had it then it would not be spreading so rapidly!'

'I'm quite all right, Mrs Dennison, thank you, only a little tired.'

In point of fact, Beth was fairly sure that she did have the virus. She had not been well for days, but no work, no pay, and the rent had to be paid. She could not afford time off work now that her allowance had been stopped.

After looking at her with deep suspicion for a moment, Mrs Dennison walked away, her fashionably coiffured head held at a disapproving angle, and Beth surrendered to her innermost urges and pulled a face at her as she left.

She was startled to find that this did not go unobserved. There was a man watching her little impoliteness. He was standing outside, looking through the window, and his dark eyes were so intense that Beth actually jumped.

With more books in her arms, she hastily fled to the back of the shop, praying that it was not some acquaintance of Mrs Dennison who was about to come and report her, and her heart began to beat very fast when she heard the door open and close again. She lingered. That was permissible. Mrs Dennison could see the whole of the shop from her position at the other end; there were huge security mirrors.

It had been strictly drilled into Beth from the very first that this was an establishment of the highest quality and that the customers were not under any circumstances to be pressurised; discreet assistance when required only. She behaved discreetly and stayed where she was. There was a difference between discreet behaviour and actually hiding, however, and soon she had to come out to collect more books.

He was browsing. His dark eyes flashed to hers as she walked to the table, but she looked away very quickly and stood sorting out the next pile of books. She had not had the chance to observe him closely, but he seemed to be very tall, well dressed, the sort of man who could afford to buy here.

It may have been the fright he had given her, or the fact that she suddenly felt very hot, but a wave of nausea washed over her and she felt very light-headed. She put her hands flat on the table for a moment, her eyes closed, but that only made things worse and with a great effort she stood upright before the whole shop began to spin round and she slid to the thickly carpeted floor in a faint.

She came round in the middle of what appeared to be a crisis. Mrs Dennison was kneeling on the floor beside her and so was the tall, dark-eyed man.

'I *knew* she was looking strange. This is just how the virus acts! Now I'll have to get her home, and how I'm going to do that I can't think. Really, I just can't leave the shop!'

'Do not worry, *madame*. My car is parked just around the corner. I will take *mademoiselle* home.'

'Oh!' Beth could hear the suspicion in Mrs Dennison's voice. 'Well, I'm sure it's very kind, but I can't just hand a young girl over to a stranger. I mean one hears so many dreadful things!'

'That is very wise, *madame*, your caution does you credit. However, you may set your mind at rest. I am Mademoiselle Craig's guardian. I am here in England to see her. Naturally I will take her home.'

Mrs Dennison was now in a quandary. For the first time in living memory she was silent, brightening up when she saw that Beth's eyes were open.

'Oh, Elizabeth!' Her exclamation of relief brought the dark eyes of the man back to Beth but she avoided them by looking the other way. 'I do have to be careful, dear. Tell me, do you have a guardian?'

'Theoretically, yes,' Beth admitted, her voice a little weak. 'He's a Frenchman. Monsieur Vernais.'

The dark-eyed stranger slid his hand into his pocket and pulled out a passport, flicking it open under Mrs Dennison's nose.

'Gaetan Vernais, *madame*, as you see. Now, if you do not mind, I will see to it that Mademoiselle Craig gets home safely.'

Beth was not able for the moment to react at all. She really felt dreadfully ill and she could see that Mrs Dennison was thankful to have the Frenchman taking the responsibility. He helped Beth to her feet, sitting her in a chair before leaving her to fetch his car.

She had a peculiar trapped feeling, not at the moment with enough energy to fight her way out of this situation. The moment that she got to her bedsit, though, she would be on home ground, then she would take charge of her own affairs. At the moment she was feeling too ill and not a little stunned.

She had no reason to be anything but infuriated by Gaetan Vernais. She had faced a lot of trouble because of him, and if now he thought that she would greet him in any way other than with annoyance he was very much mistaken. He was not quite as she had imagined him. Although she still had not had a very good look at him she knew one thing for sure: he was much younger than she had thought.

He was back within minutes, his hand beneath her arm, guiding her out of the shop.

'Don't come back until you're quite better, Elizabeth!' Mrs Dennison said in a voice that was more threatening then concerned, but Beth had no chance to speak.

'Mademoiselle Craig will not be back at all, *madame*!' the Frenchman said firmly. 'In future she will be living in Paris. If you owe her any wages, you may keep them in lieu of notice.'

'But...!' Beth tried to intervene, her voice more than a little alarmed, but she was given no opportunity to decide her own fate.

'Come!' He ushered her through the door, across the pavement and into his car, a great silver-grey Rolls-Royce, sitting her firmly in the passenger seat and pulling off at once.

'I—I live at the...'

'I know where you live, *mademoiselle*!' he said shortly. 'I have been there already today, that is how I discovered where you were working. You may rest. I am quite capable of driving us there!'

Beth fell silent. She was not nearly as confident as she appeared to be. In her daily life she put on a face that fooled everyone, but at this moment she was not quite capable of it. Silence seemed to be a good idea. In any case, she was shivering although the car was warm and comfortable.

He turned into the street, stopping at the house where she had the second-floor front bedsit, and it was clear that the situation did not amuse him at all. The street seemed especially dark tonight and Beth shivered, pulling her jacket closely around her,

knowing that it would be cold in the flat. She was
cold too and trembling, more from the virus, she reminded herself, than from the thought of the tall, dark
man who helped her to the front door, his hand un-
necessarily hard on her arm.

In the end, it was he who opened the front door,
taking her key impatiently from her after her third
attempt to insert it. She noticed with a new wave of
alarm that he slid it into his pocket with no offer to
return it to her, and it was with relief mixed with fear
that she opened her own door, getting the key in first
time now and stepping inside, switching on the
overhead light.

'*Dieu!* It is colder in here than outside!' he grated
from the doorway. 'No wonder that you are ill! Pre-
sumably you are accustomed to handling that ancient
contraption of a gas fire? Turn it on! Any attempt
on my part to do so would probably result in the whole
building being exploded!'

Beth found herself obeying meekly, her head
swimming as she bent. She told herself that this sub-
servient reaction was due to her illness and nothing
more, but truly, he was alarming her very much. To
call his attitude severe would be a great understatement. Still, she couldn't put off facing him any
more. She had ducked out of his way in the shop,
avoided looking at him on the way here but he had
to be faced now, even though she knew that she would
be looking at her only real enemy in the whole world.

In her mind, she had always imagined him to be
someone of her Uncle John's age, a man in his sixties,
someone perhaps balding, running to fat. She had
imagined him as ugly, cruel, mean and vicious, and
for a few seconds her mind refused to believe what
she saw as he stood tall and angry in the doorway.

He was a superb male animal, even her innocent mind saw that, and he looked just about ready to spring on her in a fury like a dark, sleek panther. His hair was thick and black, a little longer than she would have thought someone with such beautifully tailored clothes would wish it to be, and his eyes beneath winged brows were glitteringly dark.

He was deeply tanned, and there was a power about his broad shoulders and chest that spoke of tightly packed muscles just below the surface of the expensive clothes. His height seemed to be filling the doorway, his anger filling the room, and she simply stared mutely, her eyes running over him from the black trousers and black high necked sweater to his grey tweed jacket that only emphasised the darkness of the rest of him. He made an alarming picture, like the Prince of Darkness or his emissary, and she gulped in growing fear.

He was not old at all, her mind assured her in some astonishment. He was no more than thirty-two or three, but that didn't seem to help at all. There was no pushing this man aside or ordering him out. He could probably snap her neck with one powerful hand, and he looked just about ready to do it.

'I—I . . .' She swayed on her feet and he was against her instantly, terrifying at close quarters.

'Sit down, *mademoiselle*!' He lowered her into the only armchair in the room and she sank down thankfully. 'I will make a drink for you if you will tell me where you keep the coffee.'

'I don't think there's any left,' she said apologetically, half rising. 'I usually have tea,' she added quickly, not wanting him to do anything for her, but he motioned her back to the chair with an imperious gesture, his eyes seeking out the cupboard she had indicated.

'I have never made tea, but I imagine that I will be able to master the general principles,' he assured her sardonically. 'You will be able to tell me your English opinion of the result.'

She watched him like someone in a daze. If she had been well, if she had been herself she would probably have found it quite hilarious to see a very well dressed Frenchman studiously spooning tea into a teapot and making up a tray for his defiant ward. At the moment, though, she felt that it would only serve to increase his already obvious anger.

'It—it's very good. Thank you.' She sipped the tea as he handed her a cup, grateful for the hot, sweet drink, still shivering though.

He looked impatiently round and pulled the cover off her neatly made bed, wrapping it around her shoulders, leaving her arms free, and she sat wide-eyed in her cocoon of warmth as he grasped a high-backed chair as if it were cardboard, swinging it round with its back to her and straddling it, his arms folded along its straight back as he looked her over mercilessly.

She really felt like a small and valueless object under a microscope as his eyes raked slowly over her, missing nothing. From her long and heavy thick gold hair with its tightly bound braid, over the pale, almost translucent skin of her face which held not one vestige of colour, to her soft and trembling lips, his eyes wandered irritably. His gaze lingered on her rather outlandish clothes and all she could do was to gaze helplessly back.

Many times she had paced this room, rehearsing bitterly the things she would say to this man should they ever meet, but not one word came to her head now. In the first place, he was not the man she had imagined and built her bitterness around, and also, his whole presence frightened her. He was shockingly masculine, his eyes pitilessly intent, holding her grey eyes with no mercy in their dark depths.

'You will now explain to me, *mademoiselle*, why you felt it necessary to refuse the offer of my protection and why you choose to disobey and disregard your uncle's last wishes!'

'I do not need a guardian, Monsieur Vernais,' Beth said quietly, her eyes on her clenched hands. 'In England, a person is of age at eighteen. I am nineteen and a half, one could say almost twenty. I could marry, have children, do exactly as I please in that direction and it would be permissible in the eyes of the law.'

'Possibly!' he said scathingly. 'In your particular case, however, it would be breaking the terms of both your uncle's and your parents' will. You would be unable to claim your inheritance until you were thirty-five and would therefore be as penniless as you so clearly are now. Rather a long time to wait when you merely need to follow the terms of your uncle's will until you are twenty-one! If you wish to marry and have children then I am afraid that it, too, will have to wait. You cannot do either without my approval, and I most certainly do not approve!'

'I do not intend to marry and have children, *monsieur*!' Beth said spiritedly.

'That is fortunate, *mademoiselle*, as you are obviously still a child in your outlook!' he snapped. 'You are not accustomed to this way of life, to living in these circumstances!' His long fingered hand swept the room. 'It is outrageous that you have chosen to live like this!'

'There is nothing wrong with this place, *monsieur*!' Beth said as heatedly as she could manage. 'It is a perfectly normal place to live, and in any case, accommodation is very expensive in London. I am perfectly comfortable and happy here! My wages are not very high, but with my allowance I would have been quite well off. You probably remember though that you stopped my allowance!'

'It was not only my right to stop your allowance but my duty!' he grated savagely. 'You saw fit to disregard the provisions that had been made for your comfort and safety, and short of dragging you to Paris by your long hair there was nothing else that I could do!'

'You could have left me alone!' Beth said hotly, the effort making her begin to cough. He waited until the spasm of coughing was over, but even then he had to wait further. Beth was not finished with him. 'You made no effort to get to know me, to consider my wishes! I have been told what to do and how to do it for the whole of my life; now, I am on my own!'

'Obviously, *mademoiselle*!' he shot out sarcastically. 'You are ill, with no one to care, you were working when you should clearly have been tucked up in your bed, you are heiress to thousands and you are living here.' His eyes said, 'and looking like that', but he kept that to his scathing gaze.

'I have told you that I am happy and comfortable here, *monsieur*!' she said tightly, her eyes hot with tears of frustration. 'And if I were not, it would be your fault!'

'Correction, *mademoiselle*! It is your fault!' he bit out sharply. 'You are in this situation because of your stubborn refusal to agree to plans made for you by caring adults. In my house in Paris there is every comfort that you could wish for, a standard of living that you are accustomed to, suitable companions should you wish to choose friends who do not race through the streets on motorbikes!'

'There is nothing wrong with my friends!' Beth said sharply, 'and how did you know where I was working?'

'I was here earlier in the day, *mademoiselle*, and no doubt you remember that you have a neighbour who occupies the room opposite. She was quite willing to talk to me,' he finished smugly.

'I bet she was!' Beth snapped, her grey eyes raking over him in their turn from the long, powerful legs to the handsome, arrogant face.

'Tiens!' he blazed angrily. 'In France, it is not considered proper for a young girl to speak like that!'

'From what I have seen on my frequent visits to your country with my uncle, *monsieur*,' Beth answered sharply, 'young girls have a great deal of freedom and speak as they choose. They seem also to behave as they choose.'

'Not if they are from a good family, *mademoiselle*,' he assured her angrily. 'No young girl in France behaves with indiscretion if she is well brought up. You come from a very good family!'

'I am not a young girl, *monsieur*,' Beth reminded him with some heat, 'and I do not come from a family at all. I come from a school. It may have been one of the best schools but it was still only a school.'

Unexpectedly, he was silent, his face not quite so furious. It seemed suddenly to dawn on him that she was utterly alone, had been alone for years in actual fact. Unexpectedly too, Beth found her eyes filling with tears, and crying was the last thing she intended to do right now, but she was not used to battles, not used to putting up a fight against an aggressive man.

She did not feel well either, in fact, she was feeling worse by the minute. In spite of the gas fire and the cover she was still cold and she was hungry. He was silent, but she refused to look up at him and finally he said in a quiet voice. '*Eh bien!* It is time then, *mademoiselle*, that you did have a family, and it appears that, with your uncle dead, the responsibility of providing you with a safe home background rests with me.'

Anything that Beth would have said remained unuttered, because at that moment there was a sharp knock on the door and Gaetan Vernais moved with the litheness of a great cat to swing the chair free and aside, opening the door with almost no break in his smoothly co-ordinated movements.

'I thought I heard . . .' Her landlady, Mrs Bateman, stood there, very prim in her dark dress, her eyes startled as she gazed up at the lean, towering height of the Frenchman. 'Miss Craig!' she continued in her most righteous voice. 'I've told you before, no men in your room!'

There was a brief silence as the black eyes of Gaetan Vernais moved over Beth and then he turned back to the door.

'Do not be alarmed, *madame*,' he said stiffly. 'I do not come into the category that you so clearly mean. I have come to collect Mademoiselle Craig and take her to Paris. I am her guardian, *madame*, and if you would kindly prepare any bill for her rent, I will pay you now. She is leaving tonight!'

'Well . . . there's usually a month's notice required . . .' Mrs Bateman managed, staggered by events, while Beth sat almost open-mouthed, stunned by the Frenchman's high-handedness.

'I will give you the necessary money in lieu of notice, *madame*,' he said smoothly, 'anything else that is needed, too. Perhaps in return you would be good enough to throw out anything that Mademoiselle Craig decides to leave behind? We will not have the time.'

'Yes, well—er—yes.'

'Merci, madame.' He dismissed her politely and firmly, closing the door and turning angry dark eyes on Beth.

'You appear to be living in a manner that would have greatly displeased your uncle, *mademoiselle,* since she feels it necessary to remonstrate with you so speedily and vigorously!'

'It's in the terms of the letting,' Beth said with acute embarrassment. 'This is the only time she has ever heard a man's voice in here, because there has never been one.'

She had jumped up in agitation and both of them turned startled eyes to the door as yet another knock echoed in the room. With an angry mutter, Gaetan Vernais pulled the door open to stare with annoyance at the second visitor.

It was Carl Glover standing in the passage outside in his black leathers, his motorcycle helmet under his arm. He too looked annoyed as he took in the height and power of the Frenchman.

'The old dragon at the shop said that you'd left with a man. Who is this guy, Beth?'

'He—he's my guardian.' Clearly the Frenchman was not about to help. He looked ready to explode with rage.

'Your guardian! Pull the other one!' Carl was beginning to look really nasty and Beth hurried forward, stepping outside and closing the door on the furious face of Vernais before he could stop her.

'It's true, Carl! He's come to take me to Paris. I told you about him ages ago!'

'I thought you were spinning a yarn! You're not going, for God's sake? What do you want with a guardian at your age?'

'It was in my uncle's will,' Beth sighed defeatedly, knowing deep down that she had already partly accepted the idea. The words that her clearly bad-tempered guardian had snapped at her since they had come back to her room had begun to take effect. She was alone, prey to any misfortune. 'He's told the landlady that I'm leaving and now I'll have lost my room. Mrs Dennison at the shop was told too that I wouldn't be coming back.'

'Why the hell did you let him?'

'I feel ill, Carl! It's the virus. I can't seem to stand up for myself.'

'I'll stand up for you then!' he said rather boldly, considering the power of the French fiend who waited in her room. She did not want more trouble than she already had.

'No! Maybe I should go for a while. It will be a holiday and it will get me my allowance back. I'll talk him round when I feel better,' she added with a feeling of hysteria that she should even imagine such a thing possible with someone like that.

'That is enough time for you out in this cold passage, *mademoiselle*!' The door shot open and she was pulled firmly back into the room. 'She will write to you from Paris, no doubt!' he said with a look that dared any argument from Carl. 'Goodnight, *monsieur*!'

He slammed the door and turned furiously on Beth.

'I can see, *mademoiselle*, that your unfortunate landlady has good cause to complain! That young man obviously knew the way to your room!'

'Of course he did, he helped me to move in here! Mrs Bateman was standing watching all the time, though! He couldn't even have got into the house if you hadn't left the door downstairs unlocked! You've got my key! You left it open! Nobody has ever been here before!'

She was dizzy with standing up, cold, hungry and shaking and to her horror, she suddenly burst into tears, covering her face with her hands to shut out the sight of him.

She was stunned by the soft warmth of the deep voice so recently violent, and too bemused to put up any resistance as two strong arms drew her to the power of his hard chest.

'Come, Elizabeth. In my anger and frustration, I have misjudged you. Do not cry. We will sort you out and then things will not seem so bad, eh?' He tilted her face, wiping her tears with a large white handkerchief from his pocket before drawing her head back to his shoulder, his warm hand beginning to massage the back of her neck. 'You must come with me. *Mon Dieu*, you are too slender, too light! A strong gust of wind would blow you into the air and out of sight. It is surely only the weight of this beautiful hair that holds you to the ground. You know that you are not well, and who will care for you? That fierce old woman who recently knocked so violently on your door?'

His hand was wonderfully soothing on her nape and she found herself nestling into his warmth. 'I will help you to pack and we will be off to Paris within the hour,' he said, a satisfaction in his voice as he felt her tight body relax against him.

'I can't! I don't want to!' She drew back, stiffening like an alert animal scenting danger, but he caught her shoulders in his strong hands and looked down at her seriously.

'I think that you must, Elizabeth,' he said. 'I cannot leave you here. You are my responsibility and I intend to carry out my promise to your Uncle John no matter

what protests you make. You know perfectly well that
you should not be here, alone. At this moment you
seem to be incapable of even standing unaided. You
need to be looked after, even when you are well. Put
aside your resentment. Two years will pass very
quickly and then you will be a very rich young lady
with a polish that you will get in Paris. You will be
more mature, more capable of striking out on your
own.'

'It's not two years,' Beth corrected with still the
snatch of a sob in her voice. 'It's a year and a half.'

'*Eh bien!* A year and a half.' His long, mobile lips
twisted in wry amusement. 'You have your prison
sentence worked out exactly. Give it a try!'

'You don't understand, do you?' she said with a
little sigh. 'All my life, people who did not particularly care for me have been telling me what to do. For
the first time ever, I have freedom. You've come to
take that away from me.'

He looked down at her steadily, his dark eyes
thoughtful. 'I confess, Elizabeth, that I had not
thought of it like that at all. Your Uncle John cared
for you,' he added with a soft reproof, and she
nodded.

'Yes, he was a wonderful man, taking me on like
that, but I saw him so rarely. He was too busy, that's
why I was always in school. I'm free now.'

'Do you call this freedom?' he said quietly. 'What
are you free to do? Free to become ill while nobody
cares? Free to be in danger? I will not offer that kind
of freedom to you in Paris. I wish to take care of
you.'

'But why? I'll only be a nuisance.'

His glance softened and he pulled her slowly close,
his eyes flashing over the astonishing gold of her hair
and her pale, anxious face.

'I will not permit you to be. We will come to some kind of understanding, believe me.' She did!

'I—I won't fly to Paris!'

She had silently admitted almost from the first moment that she had seen him that her rebellion was over. She felt too ill to fight any more, and in any case, there were lots of times when she was lonely. Already she felt a kind of connection with this man, even if irritation was the only thing that would bind them together. She wanted someone of her own, someone to talk to, to share her worries, even to tell her what to do sometimes.

'You will not be asked to fly,' he answered, his satisfaction at her surrender very clear. 'I have my car, as you surely noticed. As I have had a considerable amount of travelling to do since I traced you, I thought it best to have my own car.'

'How did you find me?' Beth asked, sitting down as soon as he released her, her legs being too shaky to hold her upright.

'You wrote to your headmistress, finally,' he reminded her with a return to quiet accusation. 'She had the good sense to contact me.'

'Were—were you looking for me?' Somehow the thought heartened her. She had thought that he had just stopped her allowance in a fit of rage and had intended to let her starve to death or whatever she chose. He gave her a wry glance.

'*Oui, mademoiselle,* I was looking for you!'

Beth flushed and looked away, realising that she should have expected it. Miss Rogers would have been worried about her, it was obvious that she would have contacted him. Maybe she had deliberately overlooked it, maybe she had wanted to be caught? It mattered little now. This man was in charge of her life for many long months and the idea of trying to get round him and then come back was really only a wild thought.

He lifted her suitcase effortlessly from the top of the wardrobe.

'Change into trousers. It is warm in the car, but ports are bleak places at the best of times.'

'I haven't many clothes to take,' she murmured quietly but he continued to move around the room efficiently, taking complete charge now that she had given in.

'I cannot say that I am alarmed at that,' he said in a sarcastic murmur, glancing at her clothes. 'Provided that you have some jeans and a warm sweater for now, everything else will sort itself out. If you do not feel up to packing your clothes, I will do it for you.'

'No!' She stood quickly on decidedly shaky legs and he glanced wryly across at her.

'What else do you wish to take?' His eyes were on the many books that brightened the room.

'I want to take those, and my pictures!' She was half expecting that he would tell her to leave them to be thrown out but he did not. His eyes were on the framed photographs of her Uncle John and the couple who were laughing out at him from an older framed photograph, her mother and father, indescribably young to have been dead for so long.

'I will try to get a few boxes from your landlady. You may change while I am out.'

'Thank you, *monsieur*.' She could not help the slight resentment that coloured her voice at his overbearing attitude, and he glanced at her warningly, one dark eyebrow raised.

'Do not delay, *mademoiselle*! I shall not be long and I do not intend to wait outside in the cold passage.' To be certain of that, he took the door key with him and Beth hurried. By the time he came back she was dressed in faded but clean blue jeans and a thick red sweater, and her dark blue jacket was ready to be picked up. He looked pleased to see this change of outfit, and also to see her methodically packing her one suitcase.

He took off his jacket and looked more alarming than ever as he crouched down to pack the books, his brown hands precise and efficient, but Beth was pleased to see that he handled her precious photographs with great care.

CHAPTER TWO

SHE had never been manipulated so smoothly and subtly, Beth thought later as she sat in the car waiting for him to close the boot. The hour was by no means up and yet she was changed, packed, her things boxed and carried downstairs and a bewildered Mrs Bateman had been paid and left to clear up whether she wanted to or not.

'Good! We go at last!' he said with satisfaction as he slid into the car. 'Fasten your seat-belt, *mademoiselle*, and we will be on our way.'

She tried to but it defeated her, and after watching her struggles for a second he leaned across and fastened it himself. He smelled good, a clean and slightly tangy smell that she knew was aftershave, and his hands were deft and quick. For a brief second, his arm pressed against her small, rounded breasts and an odd feeling shot through her that frightened her enough to have her drawing back tightly against the leather seat.

He felt her reaction and glanced at her quickly, his face puzzled in the soft internal light of the car.

'I have hurt you, Elizabeth?' he asked, a frown creasing his broad forehead.

'No! No, Monsieur Vernais,' she said a little too quickly, and he sat upright, his eyes glancing at her sideways as he started the engine, flicking off the internal light, plunging them into the peace and luxury of the darkness.

24

'I do not wish you to call me that,' he said firmly.
'Although I have taken on the responsibility for you,
I do not require this strict formality. You will call me
Gaetan.' She couldn't think of an answer and after a
brief pause he said quietly, 'You are Elizabeth, which
to my mind is a beautiful name, but few people call
you that, do they? You seem to be called Beth and I
will call you that too, if you have no objections.'

'I have no objections, Monsieur Vernais,' she said
dully. She was already drowsy, the luxurious warmth,
the smooth ride and the comfort of the seat seeping
into her cold and aching body.

'Gaetan!' he corrected, glancing sideways at her
when she merely murmured, 'Yes.' She was almost
asleep, delicately childlike, the heavy braid of golden
hair pulled forward over her shoulder. Now that she
was wearing jeans, the long and outrageous skirt discarded, her violently bright blouse replaced by a high-
necked sweater, she looked younger than ever. There
was no defiance now on her softly beautiful face, and
for a moment he considered stopping the car so that
he could look at her without the shimmering grey of
her eyes looking defiantly back at him. He grunted
irritably and drove on in the darkness.

The crunch of tyres on gravel and bright lights pen-
etrating the car brought Beth from her light doze as
the car stopped, and she turned anxiously as she recognised a very smart and expensive hotel.

'Why have we stopped?'

'I remembered that you had not eaten,' he said,
apparently amused at the sound of her sharply anxious
voice. 'Neither have I. Here will do. You know the
place?'

'No, but I can see what sort of place it is. I can't
go in there, *monsieur*!'

'Gaetan,' he corrected mildly. 'And why can you not go in there, Beth? It does not appear to be a place of ill-repute.' He was laughing at her, even though his face was perfectly serious and she flushed swiftly.

'I cannot go in there, *monsieur*,' she said with determination, 'because I am not dressed for the occasion.'

'Fine feathers do not make fine birds,' he reminded her coolly.

'Perhaps not, *monsieur*,' she retorted, 'but dingy feathers make dingy birds!'

'You prefer to go hungry?' He looked at her coldly, seeing that he had no way of getting her inside unless he was prepared to take her in under his arm. 'Very well, *mademoiselle*,' he said evenly, taking his cue from her and returning to formality. 'We will proceed!'

He drove off, and for a moment she almost relented. She was hungry and the thought of food made it even worse, but she was deeply sure that he was either laughing at her inside or being cruel in order to keep her firmly to heel, so she said nothing. She was surprised therefore when a few miles further on he drove into the car park of a pleasant-looking country inn and stopped the engine.

'A dingy hostelry for a dingy bird,' he explained smoothly when she looked at him questioningly. 'This place I do know. I have eaten here before and the food was good. Come, Beth, I have no wish to see you collapse, and the lights are low, I assure you.'

He got out and came around to help her, urging her forward, his hand lightly on her shoulder. 'Be easy,' he remarked in an amused voice. 'Nobody will notice that you are not in a ball gown.'

'I don't need...!' she began in a quiet but irritated manner, but he interrupted speedily.

'I know exactly what you need, and that is why I am taking you to Paris. Inside out of the cold!' he ordered, pushing her forward. *'Courage, ma fille!'*

Wonderful, she thought angrily. He intended to treat her like a child! Even so, she was grateful for the hand that squeezed her shoulder encouragingly and reassuringly as she hesitated in the lighted doorway.

In the morning sunlight, Beth looked out of the window with interest as they left Calais and headed for the motorway. She had been here often before on her visits to France with her uncle and it did not seem to have improved much. The road from the port was still very bad and very crowded even in March and it took all Gaetan's attention to negotiate the narrow, rutted roads.

The previous evening still lingered in her mind but she was feeling a little better, and he had been extremely kind, she had to admit that. When they had left the small hotel where in spite of her hunger Beth had found it difficult to eat at all, they had driven straight to Dover, and although she had been able to keep her eyes open until they were on the ferry, once settled in a seat, she had fallen asleep.

She had awakened startled in a few minutes to find Gaetan was watching her closely and that she had slipped down in her seat uncomfortably.

'Do not be so jumpy,' he cautioned softly as she stared at him wide-eyed. 'Having gone to such lengths to find you I am not about to drive off the ferry at Calais and leave you.'

She shivered, her face very pale, and he reached out, pulling her against his shoulder, settling her comfortably with his arms around her, ignoring her anxious murmur.

'You do not look at all well. You will be more comfortable here. A night crossing is boring and you can catch a little sleep. It will be daylight when we reach France, and then we will press on straight home.'

Home! It sounded comfortable and safe. He seemed comfortable and safe, and after a few minutes she relaxed, resting against him until drowsiness overtook her again, sleeping deeply with his arm firmly around her.

Now they were speeding on into a new life for her as, with the motorway reached, Gaetan breathed a sigh of relief and let the beautiful car have its head like a thoroughbred horse. She had never been in such luxury. Even with all his wealth, her Uncle John had not surrounded himself with such things, and she had never been close to a man like Gaetan Vernais either.

'Have you any children, Gaetan?' she enquired shyly, using his name for the first time. It seemed stupid to be continually formal with someone who had held her sleeping against him for the time of the crossing, and in any case, it was not that he was in any way old. He was merely forbidding for most of the time.

'None that have been brought to my attention,' he said, glancing at her with a wicked gleam in his eyes. 'I am not married, Beth.'

'Oh!' She blushed at his remark, wishing she had stayed with formality. Now she didn't know what to say at all.

'I remember your uncle saying that you speak French very well,' he said after a minute of silence when her discomfort grew.

'Yes, I can manage quite well.' She hadn't spoken French for over a year, but she had been to France so many times and her uncle had insisted that she speak in French when they were here, forcing her to make conversation with people even when she didn't want to. She was glad of that now.

'You will need to speak in French all the time, even during your lessons now,' he said rapidly in French, and she answered in the same language without even thinking. Her mind was alerted to something else entirely.

'Lessons? I don't understand quite what you mean, *monsieur*.'

'Naturally, you will want to continue your studies. I understand that you are very clever, verging on the brilliant. You have passed many examinations with ease and yet you have not availed yourself of the chance to go to either of the great English universities. It does not matter, however, there are also great universities in France, you may go there. Your French is excellent and from now on we will speak in French all the time in order to improve it further before the new university year begins.'

'I do not intend to go to any university, *monsieur*!' Beth said sharply. 'Had I known that this was your intention, I would not have come with you, even though you had already lost me my job and my flat!'

'I would advise you to keep your temper, *mademoiselle*!' he warned with equal sharpness. 'You may have noticed that I have a temper of my own, and it would be better if we were to come to some sort of a truce, otherwise, our lives are likely to be stormy for the duration of your—sentence!'

'Don't worry, *monsieur*,' Beth said coolly. 'I will hardly ever speak, especially if you pursue this idea of university! I will not be ordered about!'

'It comes to my mind, *mademoiselle*,' he said coldly, 'that some of the time you will be lying across my knee as I beat some courtesy into you!'

'You wouldn't dare!' She looked across at him with her head tossed high and his eyes flared over her too slender form and her flushed, delicate cheeks.

'The thought grows by the minute, *mademoiselle*,' he assured her with a wry twist to his mouth. 'You are in France now, under my care. Discipline will be as strict or as lenient as I think necessary!'

'Discipline! I am grown up, *monsieur*!'

'At the moment, *mademoiselle*, I very much doubt that. You are a rebellious teenager, nothing more! The idea of spanking you into obedience has growing possibilities. Beware!'

She looked away from the black and gleaming eyes and stared straight ahead. Once she was feeling better, she would ignore him. He had brought her here when she did not want it, had caused upheaval in her life, she would remain only as polite as was necessary to have her own way.

She remained stubbornly quiet and he seemed content to ignore her. She was quivering with anger inside. He might have succeeded in getting her here but she had plans of her own, and they could be summed up very quickly: she intended to go back to England long before her time was up.

The satisfaction that the thought gave her was somewhat marred by the memory of how good he had been to her on the journey, as if he really cared about what happened to her. She was being driven to a luxurious house where every care would be given to her, where she would not be obliged to go to work when she felt ill. It had been good to feel his hand on her shoulder when she was nervous. It had felt as if she had someone of her own. She glanced across to apologise, but his dark, forbidding face took her courage away. She was planning to battle with this man. It would not be easy, especially when his frequent and unexpected acts of kindness could undermine her determination.

She closed her eyes, pretending to sleep, drifting back to the time when her life had been dramatically changed. She had been eight years old when her parents had been killed in an air-crash while she was staying with her Uncle John, and then she had been a happy but shy child. Even now, she remembered the misery and her Uncle John's blundering attempts to comfort her. He had been her only remaining relative, her mother's brother, and even then, she knew in the back of her mind that she would not be able to stay with him for ever. He was in the Diplomatic Service and travelled widely, a confirmed bachelor, so she had not been surprised when after only a few weeks he had told her worriedly that she would have to be sent to a school as a boarder.

That was when she had gone to St Margaret's, the school where she was to spend the next ten and a half years of her life, a place where she had learned to distance herself from a seemingly uncaring world. Unless she was on holiday with Uncle John, she rarely left the school grounds. At first, she had been invited out to the homes of friends, but she could never invite them back and finally she had refused invitations altogether.

She had been more than old enough to leave and had intended to leave that autumn when her uncle had died so unexpectedly. She was going to live in his house, work from there, be free at last. The will, however, had stipulated that the house be sold, the money held on trust for her with the remainder of his wealth, and she discovered to her horror that she had a guardian. She had taken her freedom anyway, refusing to go to France, moving into London and getting a job.

Gaetan Vernais had acted swiftly, well within the terms of his guardianship. He had cut off her allowance. She knew too, although he had not mentioned it, that he could also take steps to withhold her inheritance if she did not follow his wishes. Deep inside, she knew that he would do whatever he felt was right. He would carry out his obligations with no regard for her wishes. She would have to stay in Paris. To continue to defy him was really madness. There was no hope of victory. The time would pass. Time had passed before.

Before they reached Paris, the car swung away to the right and they began to skirt the city, still some miles away.

'I thought, *monsieur*, that you lived in Paris,' Beth said with a thread of anxiety in her voice that she was unable to disguise. It earned her a look of displeasure as he glanced across at her.

'Do not mistake my every action for villainy, *mademoiselle*,' he warned. 'I live in Paris, though not actually in the city itself. I have no wish to spend my life in the middle of a traffic jam, and you have yet to see how my countrymen behave when they are pressed for time. I need to be close to the city but I prefer the illusion of the countryside around me.'

Somewhat chastened, Beth held her tongue and contented herself with viewing the surroundings that were to be her home for the next year and a half. They were now driving along roads that were edged with massive chestnut trees, many of them close to bursting into blossom. The villages along the way were small and pretty and she would have liked to stop and walk for a while even though she still felt less than well. She knew, however, that such a request would be refused by her grim-faced guardian.

Most of the things about her seemed to infuriate him, and although he had shown her kindness when she needed it and had been thoughtful and considerate while they were on their journey, there was no doubt whatever in her mind that she would be an unwelcome intruder in his house and in his life. He was simply following his code of honour, keeping a promise, made no doubt long ago when her uncle's death had seemed to be unlikely before she reached the age of twenty-one.

A small shiver of fear passed over her, and her sweet mouth lost its curve. She would have to live out the time, persevere as she had always done, and she would have to try to reach some level of understanding with Gaetan Vernais because he was too much of a man to be cast aside. She feared that ignoring him would only bring on wrath, or at the very least, this disdainful silence that was beginning to hurt.

Soon they were running between long lines of poplars, and on each side she could see massive and wealthy-looking estates, but it was not until the car slowed by high, stone walls and Gaetan pressed a switch to open electronically controlled gates that she realised they had arrived. Immediately her heart began to pound.

They drove through well wooded grounds, and her first sight of the house that she was to call home for the next long months brought a lump to her throat. It was large and white, looking like the country houses that she had seen from time to time in England, with long, elegant windows, the upper ones with stone balconies, the lower ones reaching to the ground. There were pillars of slender height before the front of the house and the great oaken door was reached by a shallow flight of curving steps. It was the house of a

very wealthy man, gleaming white in the thin sunlight
and utterly unnerving.

She was greatly pleased when he drove straight
round to the back of the house and pulled into a
courtyard that contained stables and garages and she
was not unduly surprised when his arrival brought
forth a man who was clearly a chauffeur, his olive-
green leggings part of the uniform, his muscular arms
even now pulling on the matching jacket.

'You have safely returned, *monsieur*.' The man was
at the door opening it for Gaetan almost as soon as
they halted, and Gaetan got out and stretched stiffly.

'*Mais oui*, Louis, and not before time, I assure you!'
He came himself around to Beth's door, helping her
out and introducing her to the tough-looking man with
dark unruly hair. He was middle-aged, kindly looking,
and as he looked at her, Beth saw a brief flare of pity
in his eyes, a look that was instantly veiled as he came
and shook her hand.

'Mademoiselle Craig, Louis,' Gaetan said easily,
clearly on very good terms with his employee. 'She
will live here from now on, as you no doubt know
from Madame Benoir.'

'*Oui, monsieur*, we have been looking forward to
meeting her.' He gave a little bow of greeting and then
stepped back. 'I am at your service, *mademoiselle*.'

'Charming!' Gaetan breathed sardonically. 'You
have scored a hit there, *mademoiselle*. Our Louis does
not give his favours readily. He is a rogue of the worst
kind, eh, Louis?'

'Only when off duty, *monsieur*,' Louis replied with
a ready grin, and Beth learned something new about
her guardian: he was human and well liked by this
man.

As Louis delved into the boot, Gaetan led her to
the house and she soon found herself inside the back

door, moving down a long passage that ended in the
wide and charming front hall. A small and neat
woman in her late sixties appeared at the sound of
Gaetan's voice and stood beaming at them both as
Gaetan again performed the introductions.

'Mademoiselle Craig, Madame Benoir,' he said
quietly. 'This is my housekeeper, Beth, who will
comfort you, bully you and see to it that you are too
well fed.' He smiled across at Madame Benoir as she
shook her head in laughing exasperation and added,
'She is here at last, *madame*! What do you think of
her?'

'She is a very beautiful child, *monsieur*. I think we
will all be happy with her.'

'Ah! You have just said the wrong thing, *madame*,'
Gaetan informed her wryly. 'You have called
Mademoiselle Beth a child. You will now be cast into
the painful depths of silence. She will not speak to
you for a very long time.'

'I am very pleased to meet you, *madame*,' Beth said
quickly, stepping forward with a smile at the startled
elderly woman. 'Monsieur Vernais is quite wrong! I
shall talk to you until you are tired of me!' She glanced
in annoyance at Gaetan and his lips twisted in a wry
smile as he looked down at her. Then he issued very
rapid orders to the housekeeper.

'See that Mademoiselle Beth is shown to her room.
She needs a warm bath, perhaps a little soup and then
she can sleep. It has been a very tiring journey for her
and she is not well.'

'I am perfectly all right, *monsieur*!' Beth protested
sharply, turning to him quickly, her legs almost giving
way beneath her as a wave of dizziness swept over
her. His arm was around her instantly, a hard, safe
warmth, and he looked down at her pale face with a
deep frown.

'I will judge the state of your health, *mademoiselle*,' he said severely. 'Follow my instructions if you please! I will see you later!' He handed her over to Madame Benoir, who placed an arm around her and clucked like a small, worried hen as she helped her to her room.

The room at the front of the house took her breath away. Some people, it seemed, saved their wealth and gathered it around them to hoard and count. Gaetan Vernais spent his and, after her small and barely adequate bedsit, the room that was to be hers simply overwhelmed her. From the delicately draped four-poster bed to the high and elegant windows, from the soft peach of the carpet and the beautifully appointed en suite bathroom that seemed to contain everything that any woman could need in the way of toiletries, to the gilt-tinged chairs and the massive, built-in wardrobe, it stunned her, and she was hard pressed to keep her face free of open-mouthed astonishment.

She was about to snuggle down in the warm bed later, after a sweet scented bath and a delicious bowl of home-made soup, when Madame Benoir returned. After a hasty glance around to see that all was in order and that Beth was well covered in her bed, she ushered a man into the room and behind him strolled a grim-faced Gaetan, his expression showing that he was not about to give an inch in this matter.

'I have sent for the doctor, Beth,' he said firmly. 'He will look you over and make sure that you are not too ill. This is Paul Gérard who is my doctor and also my very dear friend. I will wait in the library and Madame Benoir will stay with you.'

She wouldn't have dreamed of making a scene with other people there, but her eyes were eloquent of her feelings and Gaetan left after one warning look at her. Paul Gérard was little older than Gaetan, but his

manner was strictly medical and it was only after what
proved to be a lengthy examination that he chatted
to her in a friendly way.

'So, at last, *mademoiselle*, Gaetan has his elusive
ward captured and brought to Paris. I have rarely seen
him so wild with anger as when you refused to come
here and lost yourself in the city. I trust that you do
not intend to do any such thing again? We all suffered
for it, did we not, Madame Benoir?'

'Indeed we did, doctor.' Madame Benoir smiled,
fussing around Beth and arranging the covers neatly.
'Louis was on the point of giving notice at one time.
Monsieur Vernais can be very difficult when he is in
a rage.'

'Well, he seems to be recovering from it now,' Paul
Gérard said in amusement. 'Do be good,
mademoiselle, for all our sakes.'

'I'll try, *monsieur*,' she said with a little smile, rather
worried that Gaetan was capable of even greater rage
than he had shown when he had thought that she was
in the habit of entertaining men in her room. Still, he
was extremely high-handed, and this latest act, of arranging for the doctor to come without even con-
sulting her, was a good example. When the other two
had gone and Gaetan appeared in her doorway,
looking at her with dark and glittering eyes, her annoyance showed on her face.

'You have a viral infection,' he announced quietly.
'The blood tests will tell us more and until then, you
are to stay in bed, probably for a couple of days.'

'There is no need, *monsieur*,' she said heatedly, irritated by his actions and by the level way he looked
at her as if she were a piece of furniture to be moved
around at his whim. 'I admit to being tired, but after
a small sleep I shall be quite all right and able to get
up!'

'After a small sleep, *mademoiselle*, you will take a light meal in bed and then you will take another sleep that will last until tomorrow! Even I obey the doctor's orders, and you have no alternative! When we arrived here you almost fainted again and I had to catch you. On the ferry you slept in my arms looking a small ghost. You will do exactly as you are told! I cannot do with a sick girl on my hands! I am very busy!'

Beth blushed at the reminder that she had slept in his arms, but her temper was greatly to the fore.

'I will not be on your hands, *monsieur*!' she snapped angrily. 'I will try very hard to remain unseen in your house. I realise that I am an intruder and that I shall upset the smooth running of your life to some extent, but I refuse to spend my days in bed!'

'Ma foi!' he bit out in exasperation. 'You are a small lunatic, I think! Do you imagine that I intend to keep you drugged and tied to your bed for two years?' He advanced angrily to the bed and glared down at her but once again she felt the need to answer back.

'A year and a half, *monsieur*. I am almost twenty!'

'Very well, Mademoiselle Nineteen—almost Twenty!' he rasped. 'Be your age! You know perfectly well that you are ill and that now there is absolutely no need to struggle gallantly on. You need to recover and recover you will!' He paused and hovered over her with barely controlled rage. 'As to being an intruder and remaining unseen in my house, you insult me, *mademoiselle*, and you insult too my friendship with your Uncle John!'

He was so angry that she knew that his words were all true. Somehow he got under her skin, and she felt very reliant on him when she had sworn never to be reliant on anyone again. His anger upset her even though she knew that she had brought it on almost deliberately, and tears flooded her eyes as she looked away.

'*Mon Dieu!* You think that you can insult me and snap at me like a wildcat and then hide behind floods of tears? You are more of a woman than it seems from your appearance!' He towered over her for a second and then sighed heavily, sitting on the bed beside her. 'Obey a few orders that are merely for your own good. In the morning you will feel much better and in two days, with a little luck, you will be well and exploring the house and grounds.'

She still kept her head lowered to hide her tears, very upset by the weary frustration in his voice, and he reached for her, drawing her into his arms.

'Come here, my prickly girl, come to me,' he said with a rueful laugh. 'If I am not careful, you are going to get round me with little effort.' He tilted her chin and wiped her tears with his handkerchief. 'Please do not make a habit of this,' he said with laughter in his voice, 'or you will upset the laundry arrangements of the house.'

'I—I'm sorry,' she said softly, afraid to look at him, and he drew her back to him, his hand once again soothing on her nape.

'We will forget all about it,' he promised quietly. 'You are ill. All I wish to do at the moment is to get you well. One step at a time, eh?'

She nodded against his chest, wanting to go to sleep there, yawning drowsily, her fingers unknowingly plucking at his woollen sweater as if it comforted her, and he put her back on the pillows, standing with one fluid movement, his eyes a little startled on her face when she glanced up at him.

'When we deal with your new clothes,' he remarked slowly, 'we will also deal with your night attire.' His eyes roamed over her very serviceable nightdress that covered her in almost every place. 'No doubt Paul imagines that I abducted you from an orphanage. You do not look like the heiress to thousands.'

'It was cold in my bedsit,' she said quickly, blushing under his intent gaze.

'It is warm here,' he murmured. 'We will have that nightdress framed!' His eyes lingered over her beautiful face and her heavy, golden hair and then he turned abruptly to the door. 'For now, go to sleep. I shall take a few hours' rest myself and then I am dining out. Please obey my orders and then we can get on with your future.'

He walked out and she allowed her eyes to follow his tall, athletic figure. She was a little downcast that he was going out to leave her alone so soon, but she knew that she could not expect him to interrupt his normal life for her. She was only here for a short while, to move on the very perimeter of his life, and when she had gone, he would be out of her life for ever, she out of his.

His parting shot too had made her uneasy—'we can get on with your future'; it denoted a great deal of interference, and she would not tolerate that. It was as well that he intended to get on with his own affairs and leave her to hers. All the same, she still felt the warmth where he had held her and comforted her, she still felt the touch of his hand on her nape. It was nice to have someone caring what became of her, she decided, even if that someone was a very determined and arrogant Frenchman.

She slid down in the comfortable bed and closed her eyes, and when Madame Benoir stole in a little later, she was able to report to *monsieur* that Mademoiselle Beth was sleeping peacefully and that there was a slight glow of colour in her too pale cheeks.

*   *   *

Apart from the fact that he popped his head inside the door to wish her good morning and goodnight, Beth saw absolutely nothing of Gaetan for the next two days, and by the morning of the third day she was feeling quite well and very fretful. She obeyed his orders, though, and stayed where she was, re-reading some of her books and chatting to Madame Benoir when she was not too busy.

She was brushing her long hair, sitting beside the bed feeling rather wistful, when Gaetan paid her a visit. He stood in the doorway, coming no farther in than he had ever done since her first day at the house, and she suddenly felt at a loss for words. During their stormy meeting and afterwards on the long journey to Paris, a kind of grudging relationship had grown between them. Now, after two days when she had hardly seen him, he was a stranger, and his virile presence, his aggressive good looks left her tongue-tied.

'Today you may get up and wander around the house,' he said abruptly after staring at her for a few disconcerting seconds. He glanced around the room, his eyes on her books. 'You need a bookcase in here. I am sorry. The thought had not occurred to me. There are also books in my library which will interest you as your French is so good. You may get them whenever you wish.'

'Thank you. I'll read after breakfast.' She could not think of anything to say and his eyes stayed on her for a long time, simply staring.

'No, there is something else that you must do first,' he said with no inflection in his voice that would lead her to believe that he could be sidetracked from his purpose. 'When you have had your breakfast, come down to the library. I will meet you there. Be pre-

pared to go into the city. It is not too warm either,
so wear something appropriate. I do not wish to see
you so ill again.'

'Yes.' Beth nodded and looked away. Already her
mind was sorting through her few clothes. She
couldn't think of a thing that she had that would be
appropriate for Paris on a cool day. Her few good
clothes were summer clothes, bought when she had
gone on the Continent with her uncle. Many of those
too were not now suitable, her figure had changed.

She looked up to find him still watching her and
she realised that she had gone on absent-mindedly
brushing her hair. She had retreated very often into
her thoughts while she was at school and the habit
had stuck, shutting people out. He probably thought
her very rude. She put her brush down in her lap
guiltily.

'Hmm!' Gaetan watched her for a few moments
more, his eyes going from her slender, graceful hands
to the shining fall of hair that flowed in a cascade of
gold down her back. 'You look at this moment like
a mermaid sitting there, brushing your flowing locks,
your eyes as grey and shimmering as the sea. What a
strange creature you are, *ma fille*. One wonders what
is to become of you.'

He left as silently and abruptly as he had arrived,
and Beth sat dejectedly for a moment trying to make
some sense out of his softly spoken words. That she
was a strange and unlooked-for oddity in his no doubt
glamorous life she had not the slightest doubt, and it
must have taken all his considerable determination to
follow his code of honour and bring her back here.
Well, she was here now and she would have to make
the best of it, and so would Gaetan.

Unfortunately, things did not now seem to be so clear in her mind, and her resolve to have her own way was not now so strong. It was probably the virus, she thought hopefully, and began to re-braid her hair, her mind once again on her clothing situation. She sighed and looked around the lovely room. She would not be happy to give up all this. It was not only the comfort. It was beginning to feel like home, a real home.

Finally, her mind returned to the vexing problem of clothes, and she decided that it would have to be the jeans and red sweater again. With a resigned shrug, she picked up her jacket and walked down the stairs, facing the household of Gaetan Vernais for the first time since she had come tiredly in by the back door on her arrival. She felt a great deal better, and she was ready for anything that he could throw at her. She would not give in readily as she had done before. He was absolutely nothing to her, and she would cling to any freedom that she had.

CHAPTER THREE

BETH didn't know where the library was, but the sound of voices directed her and she went forward, leaving her jacket on a chair in the hall. Her hand was almost on the door-handle when she realised that Gaetan was speaking, not to Madame Benoir but to another woman whose voice she did not know. It was not this that stopped her in her tracks though, Gaetan's words did that.

'Well, you will see her in a few minutes and you can judge for yourself.'

'But, *chéri*, cannot you give me a little clue? What does she look like? Is she clever, stupid, what?'

There was a pause and Beth realised that she was waiting with as much anxiety as the unseen woman to hear Gaetan's assessment of her. When it came, she was stunned into immobility.

'She is young, very young, tall, slender, and I suppose, to be fair, she is beautiful. She appears, however, to be filled with resentment and all of it aimed at me. I suppose that I could not have expected her to be anything but difficult, considering the life she has led, but I had hoped ... I shall need all the help I can get.'

'She is not a child, Gaetan, she is almost twenty. I have never known, *chéri*, when you treated a twenty-year-old girl as a child.'

'Beth is different! She has been buried in some school for most of her life, she had never really lived! She does not have the subtleties of a woman. You will

see exactly what I mean and you know what you are
to do today, Madeleine? Take charge fully, she is not
capable, she appears to have gone from the strictures
of school uniform to the bizarre apparel of a hippie!'

'She is stupid then, would you say?' the voice enquired mockingly, and received a growl of annoyance
from Gaetan.

'Far from it! She is highly intelligent, with enough
brilliant examination results to paper this room, apparently! What do the English call a woman like that?
A blue-stocking? Obscure people, the English!
Whatever, she is refusing to continue her education,
and what I will do with her I do not know. Today
though, my dear, you will help me out and it is up to
you to... Well try your best with her, I cannot. I really
think that she hates me.'

'One could almost feel sorry for you, *chéri*,' the
voice mocked. 'For the first time in your handsome
life, a woman hates you. Already I am on her side.'

'No doubt you will get along very well with her,
Madeleine. Madame Benoir has apparently raised her
status to that of saint, and although that rogue Louis
has seen Beth only once, he requires a daily bulletin
on her progress towards complete recovery.'

'She is going to upset your smooth and luxurious
life, Gaetan. Already I can see that. How are you
going to treat her, as a younger sister, as a child, as
a prisoner?'

'How the hell do I know?' he snapped. 'I suppose
that I should not have been surprised at her, but I
am!'

'You could have left her. She is not penniless.'

'She is John's niece and I made a promise. Neither
he nor I realised at that time that it would have to be
kept but she is here, my responsibility, and there the
matter ends.'

Beth heard nothing more. She was utterly crushed by what she had heard already, and though her mind told her that it was exactly as she had expected, she felt doubly vulnerable to have heard him confirm it. She *had* been difficult, too, and had planned to be even more difficult. Suddenly her sympathies were all with Gaetan, and she had no idea how to undo what had already happened.

He was discussing her with one of his lady-friends and normally that would have been enough to annoy her beyond words, but somehow she felt that she deserved this humiliation and she swallowed her pride, opening the door after a brief knock.

He was leaning against a long, dark desk, his face still moody, and the woman was sitting in a chair at the side of the room, her movement as she got to her feet attracting Beth's attention.

'Ah, you are here,' Gaetan murmured. His eyes skimmed over her clothes, a sudden leaping amusement in them as he noted that she had not worn a long skirt or garish blouse. 'This is Madame St Just. Madeleine, Mademoiselle Elizabeth Craig.'

'I am pleased to meet you, *madame*,' Beth said, her face still and pale as she looked at the beautiful woman opposite. Her own inadequacies were suddenly all too glaringly obvious at the side of the chic Frenchwoman. She was almost as slim as Beth herself and her eyes were as dark as Gaetan's, her hair a pale, shining blonde, skilfully arranged, and her clothes were perfect. This was what Gaetan was accustomed to. No wonder he found her odd.

'And I, *mademoiselle*, am intrigued to meet you!' She came forward and grasped Beth, kissing her on both cheeks in the French manner, and Beth was as stunned by her warmth as she was overwhelmed by her appearance,

'Such magnificent hair!' Madame St Just sighed, turning to Gaetan. '*Chéri*, I would give everything that you own to have hair like this!'

'You are blonde yourself, Madeleine,' Gaetan reminded her with a wide grin at her witticism, but she frowned and turned away with a laugh.

'Thanks to the best salon in Paris, Gaetan, as you know perfectly well. This hair is absolutely real! It is like gold-dust!'

'You embarrass Beth,' Gaetan warned as Beth's cheeks took on a rosy hue. 'You must forgive my sister, Beth,' he added with a look of amusement at Madeleine. 'She is used to being spoiled and to saying whatever comes into her mind. Maybe, after all, you will have much in common,' he added with a wry look at her. 'You will go with Madeleine today. I have too much to do to accompany you—but then I think that you will probably be better served by being with my sister than with me.'

His sister! Beth could hardly stop the sigh of relief that sprang to her lips. He had not been discussing her with an outsider. How her mind made that more reasonable she did not know but she was looking for excuses for him and it was for some reason a source of joy that this beautiful woman was not his girlfriend.

'Well, we may as well go off on our travels,' Madeleine announced crisply, pulling on her gloves and making for the door. 'We shall have lunch out, but then, I do not suppose that you will be sitting here waiting, Gaetan?'

'No. I shall be out all day. I will check your achievements later.'

'If that is a threat, *mon ami*, then you know that I do not frighten easily,' Madeleine retorted, sailing through the door and motioning a bewildered Beth to follow.

Beth turned after one startled look at Gaetan but
his voice stopped her.

'Beth, one moment.' She looked at him enquiringly
and he gave her a rueful smile. 'No questions? No
demands for explanations?'

'No, *monsieur*. I know that I am going to the city
with Madame St Just.'

'You are going to buy clothes and everything else
that you need.' He walked forward quietly. 'I must
tell you this myself. I do not know how Madeleine
would take a shot across the bows from you. If you
are going to rage, then please do it now. I have told
her to spend as much as she wishes and I can well
afford it. You may be extravagant.'

She stood still and he waited for her temper to
surface, puzzled when she simply nodded.

'No arguments, Beth?'

'No, *monsieur*.' She felt very protective towards him
suddenly, not wanting to send him off for the day
with an argument in his mind.

The idea of protecting someone so powerful and
strong suddenly struck her as being ludicrous and
brought a quirk of amusement to her lips that grew
into an enchanting smile.

Gaetan seemed to stiffen, and an odd feeling ran
through Beth that she had felt only once before, when
he had fastened her seat-belt. It brought a rush of
colour to her face and as dark eyes met grey, he threw
his head back, his eyes veiled, watching her confusion.

'So, you can smile then?' he said softly. 'Perhaps
it is a good omen. I want you to enjoy this day. I want
it to make up to you some of the things you have
missed. With a bit of luck and a lot of perseverance
we will soon have that huge wardrobe in your room
filled with beautiful clothes.' He stepped close and

took her slender shoulders in his hands. 'It will bring you closer to being...'

'Normal?' she finished helpfully, and his long lips twisted into a smile of his own, a wry smile that seemed to be self-mocking.

'Perhaps,' he agreed softly. 'We shall have to wait and see. It is up to you, *mademoiselle*.'

'I shall try then, *monsieur*,' she countered, smiling up into his face. He stared at her for a moment as if puzzled and then, as Madeleine called impatiently from the hall, he bent quickly, his lips touching her cheek.

A strange feeling shot through her like static electricity and he turned away abruptly.

'Enjoy yourself, Beth,' he said quietly. 'Off you go!'

She went on trembling legs, utterly stunned that such a brotherly and kindly kiss should have left her so unsettled. She was glad that he was not about to join them and that she would probably not see him until tomorrow. He spent much of his time away from the house, and she thought that he probably had a serious girlfriend in Paris. His sister had hinted that he was popular with the ladies.

Suddenly, she was very glad that she was his ward, his responsibility. She would not like to have that arrogant masculinity turned in her direction. She was shocked at the very thought that had somehow filtered into her mind, and she hurried after Madeleine and got thankfully into the car.

Beth was silent as they drove from the house and turned in the direction of the city, and after a while Madeleine glanced at her and then looked back at the road.

'I hope that we are going to be friends, Beth,' she said rather ruefully. 'I hear from my brother that you have the gift of silence. I do not, and it would be a very good thing if we could talk together.'

'I'm sorry, *madame*,' Beth said quickly. 'I wasn't being deliberately silent. I was—thinking, that's all.'

'I see.' Gaetan's sister laughed softly. 'Do you wish to share your thoughts or shall I tell you what is planned for today?'

'I am to buy clothes, *madame*,' Beth said softly, 'I have been told that.'

'And you are not deliriously happy?' Madeleine said in astonishment. 'I was very envious, Beth, when my brother told me to take you out and lavish money on you. He is a very generous brother but never so generous as that with me. You are to come back with everything that I think you need, and he knows that with me it will be—everything! I would think that if you are willing it would also be an idea to call me Madeleine; your polite formality makes me feel old.'

'I'm sorry,' Beth laughed. 'You're not old, in fact you're very beautiful. I'm supposed to call Gaetan by his name too, but I find it difficult.'

'He is very—*formidable*!' Madeleine agreed with a deep exaggeration. 'Even so, you should try. It will please him, and that will be a good thing for all of us.'

'So the doctor told me,' Beth sighed. 'I seem to have caused trouble even before I came here.'

'Only because you did not come,' Madeleine said emphatically. 'Gaetan and your uncle were dear friends, you know, even though there was a great age difference, and Gaetan takes his responsibilities very seriously.'

'I know,' Beth sighed, not wishing to be reminded in the least that she was merely a responsibility in his life. It would have been better if he had been her uncle's age and not so very much a male. She pulled

herself up with a start when she realised that once
again she was thinking such strange thoughts.

Once in the city and on foot, Beth found that in
spite of her original decision simply to do everything
that Gaetan wanted and to suffer this outing with no
hope of enjoyment, she was in fact more excited with
every passing minute. They walked past many shops
that she would have liked to linger inside but
Madeleine seemed to know exactly where she wanted
Beth to be, and it was not until they were outside the
most fabulous shop that Beth had ever seen that
Madeleine stopped.

Beth's eyes roved from the exquisite clothes in the
window to Madeleine's smiling face, and back again
to stare with bated breath at the dresses and suits that
were placed with a scarcity of fuss that spoke of the
very expensive. There were silver and blue awnings
over every arched window and a long canopy of the
same material and design that stretched out across the
pavement making an expensive approach to the
beautifully draped glass door. Beth's eyes moved upwards over the white front and her mouth actually
fell open as she saw the name on the building.
'Vernais'.

'It—it's Gaetan's shop?'

'Don't ever say that Beth!' Madeleine shrieked as
she burst into delighted laughter. 'This is a world-
famous salon, and Gaetan would not be very amused
to hear it called a shop.' She watched Beth's face for
a minute and then said quietly, '*Mon Dieu*, you have
not the slightest idea who Gaetan is, have you?'

Beth merely looked puzzled and Madeleine sighed
and shook her head.

'I suppose that you have not been involved much
in the world of fashion, coming as you did almost
straight from school, and it is typical of him not to

tell you. It is hard to believe at your age, when all a woman normally thinks of is clothes and her own looks, that you do not recognise his name. I had better put you in the picture, then, before we go inside. Along with Dior, Yves St Laurent and Givenchy, Gaetan Vernais is one of the most famous fashion designers in the whole world. This is but one of his salons; he has others in New York, London, Rome and Milan. You are lucky, Beth. Your guardian is the sort of man that any woman would dream of having for a friend. You have *carte blanche* in this salon. We are now about to dress you in Vernais clothes.'

'You—you mean he designs all these himself?' Beth asked breathlessly, very uneasy about stepping into this luxurious salon and more than ever aware of her own shortcomings.

'Not now,' Madeleine assured her. 'He has a whole team who design for him, but the very best he still does himself and he keeps strict control over everything. Mostly, though, now he is taken up with the business side of things. Success has its drawbacks. He works very hard. Come, let us begin.'

For what seemed like hours Beth tried on one outfit after another with Madeleine and the rather unnerving woman in charge of the salon hovering over her. It was all what *monsieur* would think, what *monsieur* would approve of, but Beth finally summoned up enough nerve to add her own thoughts and this seemed both to amuse and to please Madeleine, who was prepared finally to let her make her own choices, only becoming firm when Beth would have left the whole thing at about three changes of outfit.

When they finally left she was dressed in one of her favourites, a woollen dress and matching jacket, pale grey, almost the colour of her eyes; it was patterned with tiny flowers of pink and blue and her shoes were the palest pink of the flowers, high-heeled and elegant. The other purchases were left in piles of boxes that towered from the floor of the salon, and delivery was promised within the hour.

Her next stop was at Madeleine's own hairdresser and beauty salon, and here Madeleine confessed that this was her own idea. Apparently Gaetan had not thought of this at all. Beth was walked round and clucked over by the experts, and when they finally left there it was almost dark but Beth had watched her own transformation from a thin and uncertain, rather ungainly schoolgirl figure into that of a beautiful young woman.

'I have but one worry,' Madeleine confessed as Beth climbed happily into the car for the return trip, her newly acquired make-up case beside her with strict instructions in her mind to 'Use very little on that beautiful skin'. 'Gaetan did not tell me to get your hair cut, but you cannot wear these chic clothes with your hair to the bottom of your back, lovely though it was.'

Beth agreed. Her hair had been styled into a length just touching her shoulders, the thick and heavy fringe framing her face, and the length that had been cut off was even now in a box in the car, having been made skilfully into a hairpiece to be used to alter the style later.

'I'm sure he won't mind,' Beth ventured uneasily, not at all sure, though, and Madeleine met her eyes and pulled a small face.

'I don't see why he should but all the same, I won't stay for dinner. There are some things, my dear, that you must do alone. Letting Gaetan see the shorter hair is one of them. You look sophisticated. I'm not sure how he will take this total transformation. You look perhaps a little more hard to handle.'

Beth did not have to wait very long for Gaetan's reaction. She had hoped that he would be out as he normally was but as she crossed the hall on her way to her room he came from the library and called to her before he had even seen her.

'Beth? Come here for a moment. There is someone I want you to meet.' He stopped abruptly as he saw her, and she turned back towards him with a rapidly beating heart, telling herself that this was quite ridiculous. He had been the one to insist upon new clothes, and as to her hair, it was really nothing to do with him at all. She had let Madeleine's anxiety creep into her own attitude, and she would not allow that. She faced him with her head high, a certain amount of defiance on her face.

It was fairly dark in the hall, but to her consternation he flicked on the main lights and came forward slowly, his eyes narrowed in what might have been either concentration or annoyance, she wasn't sure which. Whatever it was, she had found a new confidence. She had spent much of that day in looking at herself in mirrors at both the Vernais salon and at the hairdressers. She did not feel any longer an ungainly and uncertain girl, and her new-found confidence showed in her reaction to this dark and intent scrutiny.

'I didn't think that you would be in tonight,' she said casually, determined not to falter under his vivid gaze, but her observation drew forth no comment whatever. He continued to stare at her, a sort of bafflement on his face that brought a further quiver of disquiet to her.

'Well? What do you think?' she exclaimed, turning slowly round as she had done for Madeleine in the salon, praying that he would say something soon before her nerve gave out.

'Delightful,' he murmured, but with a frown on his dark face that belied the words, and a wave of exasperation shot through Beth, bringing a flare of colour into her face.

'You don't really appear to think so!' she commented irritably. 'After all, the clothes are your own design, and if you don't like the way that I wear them then you should have sent me to another establishment, or left me exactly as I was!'

'As you were?' he enquired moodily and almost absent-mindedly, his eyes still taking stock of her astonishing transformation. 'I like these very well, did I not say that you looked delightful?'

'You didn't really mean it though!' she blurted out disappointedly and his eyes came back to her face.

'I am glad that you are able to read my mind,' he commented irascibly, 'it will save me the trouble of issuing orders!' His eyes held hers and, before the dark, intent gaze, she lowered her lashes and fell into silent confusion.

'I've done everything that you wanted me to do,' she reminded him quietly and he came forward, taking her arm firmly and leading her to the library.

'And several things that I did not tell you to do,' he pointed out softly. 'I am sorry, Beth, you have astonished me, but nevertheless, you look as I said—delightful. Forgive my mood, perhaps I am mourning the loss of a strange mermaid who stayed here for a while.'

There was no further chance to speak to him and, in any case, she had decided not to have any argument with him again. She had been hurt by his seemingly disapproving attitude, but a very strange change had come over her too. She suddenly felt quite at home here, no longer an intruder, and there was a great feeling of security inside her as Gaetan stepped aside and motioned her into the library. If she had to have a guardian it was better to have one who was so certain of his requirements.

A tall, good-looking young man rose to his feet as Beth entered, and Gaetan introduced him.

'This is Alain Rouselle, Beth. He is an associate of mine. Mademoiselle Craig, Alain.'

'What he means, *mademoiselle*, is that I work for him!' He came forward, taking her hand and raising it to his lips with Gallic courtliness, looking into her eyes with smiling brown gaze. 'I am enchanted, *mademoiselle*,' he murmured.

'You may join the queue!' Gaetan offered derisively as she blushed with pleasure. His hand came once again, firm and possessive, to grip Beth's arm as he led her to the settee facing Alain, sitting down beside her himself. There was a deliberately protective attitude about him that Beth could see was not lost on the visitor. The newcomer seemed to be in his late twenties, tall and well built, definitely handsome but with none of the brooding power to his face that Gaetan had. He looked as if he laughed a lot and, never having had much laughter in her life, Beth was instantly attracted to him. She met his smiling eyes with a smile of her own.

'I hear that you have been raiding the salon, *mademoiselle*,' he remarked easily, crossing one elegant leg over the other and continuing to smile at her. 'May I be so impertinent as to enquire why you chose that particular outfit?'

'I am almost afraid to answer, *monsieur*,' Beth said with a low laugh. 'Is there any rivalry in the Vernais establishment? If there is, I had better keep quiet.'

'It was almost an innocent question, *mademoiselle*,' Alain assured her with a wide smile. 'Of course, I will not press the point.'

'I decided to keep this on because I liked it so well, as a matter of fact,' Beth confessed. 'Is it one of your designs?' She was very glad that she had had a long talk with Madeleine about Gaetan's establishment. They had discussed it through the whole of their lunch time and she knew that Alain Rouselle was already making a name for himself with Gaetan's approval, and that this year he was to be allowed to release designs under his own label.

'No, *mademoiselle*,' he said with a sadly mocking frown. 'Unfortunately, you are wearing a Vernais original. You wear the raiment of your lord like a lady at a medieval tournament.'

'You are too fanciful to be real!' Gaetan growled with little humour. 'In any case, you have it wrong as usual. To be quite logical, it is I who should be wearing the lady's favour.' His tone said quite clearly that he neither expected the slightest favour from her, nor did he intend to offer any. Still, she was almost happy. For the first time in her life, she felt under a heavy protective cloak as if there was someone who cared about her. The fact that he was like a very severe older brother did not matter in the least.

'I understand that you will be taking a place at the university when term starts in September, *mademoiselle*,' Alain said, skilfully getting away from a subject that clearly irritated Gaetan, but he was still on unfirm ground without realising it. Beth tensed and felt Gaetan's tension too. For a moment all her good resolve left her. He had even told others, then, that she was to be sent to university, whether she liked it or not!

For one second she contemplated a sharp rejoinder, but her memory of Gaetan's voice as he had talked to Madeleine, the utter weariness in him at the task he had undertaken to look after her, stilled her tongue.

'Yes,' she chanted happily. 'I imagine that I shall enjoy it. It's quite exciting.' She would take this up later with Gaetan. She was not about to snub him in front of a stranger. Even that thought made her feel oddly contented. Gaetan was no longer a stranger.

He stood and walked to the drinks which were laid out on a low table at the side of the room, his back towards her.

'The same again, Alain?' he asked pleasantly, and when Alain agreed, he added softly, 'A sweet sherry, Beth?' She could hear the laughter at the back of his voice and she didn't know whether she was being offered a sweet sherry because she looked old enough now to have one or whether it was an amused comment on her sweetly accepting tone at the mention of the university.

'Thank you,' she said lightly, wondering what it would be like, and he walked across to hand it to her, his eyes still amused as she took it from him and sipped it carefully.

'It is quite a long time to September,' Alain was commenting when she finally got her beating heart under control and dared to look at Gaetan as he stood leaning casually against the fireplace, his eyes glittering and black on her face and hair. 'Would you allow me to show you some of the city before your studies become too arduous?'

She couldn't help glancing anxiously at Gaetan, but his face was utterly without expression and she knew that no help was coming from that direction.

'I really would like to, but I shall be very busy— preparing,' she murmured to Alain, hoping that she was saying the right thing. There would be enough trouble when she took up the little matter of university later.

She heard the approval in Gaetan's voice as he added his own comments.

'Beth has been away from full-time education for a year and she has also been ill. She cannot afford the time to behave as any other person of her age would behave. She is extremely clever and must not let her chances slip by.'

'I can see that she is quite content to be in the hands of a slave-driver,' Alain stated with a quick glance at Gaetan, and Beth expected some angry comment, but to her surprise Gaetan laughed.

'Do I not always slave-drive? I have not noticed any complaints from you, Alain.'

'But it is my career and I wish to learn from the master,' Alain said with a quirk to his lips. 'She is so beautiful. It is a shame to keep her locked in a room with old books.'

There was a slight irritation on Gaetan's face, and Beth chose to intervene quickly.

'Gaetan only wants what he thinks is best for me,' she stated. 'He is my guardian and I know he wants to keep me on the right road. He has taken on the duty of protecting me.'

Somehow, she didn't think that this loyal little speech had gone down too well with Gaetan for some reason, and she was very glad when he invited Alain to dinner. Right at this moment, she would have been glad to be sitting next to Madeleine with her ready tongue and her total disregard for Gaetan's finer feelings.

Gaetan's suddenly morose mood did not lighten either throughout dinner, and she found herself talking almost exclusively to Alain who insisted upon first names and kept her laughing with a series of stories and comments that helped with what could have been a very trying little dinner party.

'Well, I shall try to get you to leave the fold, Beth,' he said as she stood at the door with Gaetan to say goodbye. 'I shall ring you up and call round unexpectedly when Gaetan is out.'

'Then I shall tell Madame Benoir that you are not to be admitted,' Beth laughed, waving goodbye and stepping back into the hall with Gaetan as he closed the door. The laughter had certainly left with Alain, she thought, as Gaetan appeared to be about to walk away to the library and ignore her totally.

'Gaetan,' she said, using his name with a determined but anxious force. 'May I speak to you before bedtime?'

He turned and looked at her a trifle sourly, his eyes doing what they had been doing all evening, sweeping over her with unreadable intensity.

'You may come back into the library,' he said grudgingly. 'Is it not something that will keep?'

'I don't think so,' she said doggedly. 'I could not say it before, but I want to say it now!'

'Well, you have certainly been busy before,' he agreed, motioning her into the room ahead of him. 'I imagine that the hairdo was Madeleine's idea?' he suddenly snapped.

'Yes, but I was in full agreement with it,' she assured him, determined not to quarrel with him and wondering why he was so very touchy now. 'I couldn't very well wear clothes like this with long hair.'

'No,' he agreed with a steady look at her. 'However, your new appearance presents its own difficulties. Now that you have discarded your disguise you will need to be well protected.'

'I—I don't understand.' Beth looked at him, puzzled and worried, her puzzlement changing to acute embarrassment when he said scathingly, 'Come, you were surely not unaware of Alain's interest? I have more to do with my time than to fight off interested and panting males who are allured by you!'

'How—how can you speak like that?' Beth gasped, her face glowing pink.

'Very easily,' he jeered, 'the truth has a habit of hitting one in the eye!'

'Alain was merely being polite,' she muttered, wishing she had gone straight to bed.

'Alain is a man, and a Frenchman at that!' he rasped. 'Perhaps it would have been better if you had simply stuck to formality as you usually do with me instead of playing the hostess so very well!'

'I am well aware that Alain is a man, *monsieur*!' she snapped, slipping back into her old habits of self-defence. 'But then, so are you!'

'I am your guardian!' he pointed out with stinging reproof. 'We are talking about strangers!'

'You are also little more than a stranger, *monsieur*,' she assured him with a growing misery at this uncalled-for anger when she had been so comfortable with him earlier. 'You did not even tell me about your profession. Had it not been for Madeleine, I would have felt very foolish tonight when Alain so clearly expected me to know everything about you.'

'It seems to me,' he said with dangerous quiet, 'that you have not been interested at all in anything about me. Your sole interest thus far has been to defy me and to escape from me. I had no desire to bore you with my life history.'

'I will go to bed, *monsieur*!' she snapped. 'Goodnight!'

He reached out and grasped her shoulders, spinning her towards him, pulling her close before she could even struggle. She was trapped against his chest, her arms pinned to her sides, her startled and frightened eyes looking up into his dark, cold face before any

real fear could develop and her growing terror seemed
to amuse him greatly.

'You are frightened out of your wits,
mademoiselle,' he said in a grating but satisfied voice.
'This is what I have been trying to put to you, but it
is clear that words make little impression on you. Now
that you have changed into such a delightful and
interesting creature, you cannot expect to go unnoticed. You are beautiful. Even the addition of your
high heels makes you more available.'

'A-Available for what?' she stammered in a tiny,
scared voice.

'Available for kissing, *ma petite*,' he murmured
softly, his dark eyes roaming over her flushed and
anxious face. 'You have soft, trembling lips, a soft
and desirable body. Alain is not the only one with
eyes in his head; there will be others!'

'You—you're frightening me, *monsieur*!' Beth
gasped, as frightened by the strange excitement that
was gripping her as by anything else.

'I am trying to, *mademoiselle*,' he assured her. 'If
I am succeeding then it will all have been worth while.'

'You are succeeding,' she said fervently, her face
chalk-white. 'I believe you!'

'Not fully, I think,' he murmured. 'The lesson has
not yet finished.'

CHAPTER FOUR

HIS eyes were on her tender and parted mouth as he lowered his head, and she was powerless in his strong arms as he pulled her closer and covered her lips with his own. For a second she stiffened in terror. This was new, utterly unexpected and completely unforgivable. She tried to pull free, but his grip tightened painfully and she suddenly stopped fighting, feeling very close to fainting but tremblingly aware of feelings she had never experienced before.

Heat flooded through her, and as he felt her lack of resistance his grip on her eased and his lips began to move over hers, slowly and sensuously as his hand slid to the bottom of her back, urging her closer.

Everything inside her began to flame, and his other hand came to cradle her head, easing the strain on her neck as if he knew exactly where she hurt. The kiss deepened for a while as if he had completely forgotten the reason for it, and Beth was a trembling and unresisting pliant being in the strength of his arms, her eyes still closed, her face bewitched when he lifted his head and put her away from him a little.

'Why?' she whispered at last, her eyes great pools of silver.

'Why not?' he enquired harshly, his face still and shuttered. 'Surely it is better to have lessons from someone with whom you are completely safe than to find out the hard way from a dangerous stranger?'

'Alain only wished to take me out, *monsieur*,' she whispered with trembling lips.

'In the first instance, perhaps,' he agreed mock-ingly. 'Today you have rejoined the living. Learn that they do not all live like you.'

'And what about you, *monsieur*?' she asked tremu-lously. 'Is that how you live?'

'Not with you, *ma fille*,' he said tightly, releasing her. 'I am your guardian! However, if you continue to call me *monsieur* I may well become violent!'

'You are violent!' Beth snapped, her humiliation suddenly making itself felt as the enchantment drained away. 'And not at all to be trusted!'

He threw his dark head back and laughed, the odd tension leaving him as he indicated that she should sit down.

'You have little choice but to trust me, Beth,' he pointed out drily. 'You will find that I can be very comfortable to live with. I merely wish to have you realise the danger of youth and beauty.'

'I have a boyfriend in England, *monsieur*,' she said, untruthfully; Carl could not be called that by any stretch of the imagination. 'I—I'm quite experienced with men.'

'I do not think so.' His eyes ran over her still trem-bling form. 'I am not, after all, really so devastating, and yet you are in quite a state of nerves after one second of a warning lesson.'

'I shall not need another lesson,' Beth pointed out primly, abandoning her efforts to convince him of her worldliness. 'I learn very quickly and I shall be happy to go out only with you.'

'With me!' He looked down at her with a wry grin. 'You imagine that I will want you hanging around my neck?'

'I don't suppose so,' she said stubbornly, 'but I shall anyhow! You brought me here, you insist that this is my home and you are most certainly my guardian!'

'So you are suggesting that we are stuck with each other?'

'Yes!' Beth glared at him, having worked herself up to it she intended to have everything out once and for all. 'Now, I would like to speak to you!'

'Of course!' He sat opposite and regarded her with interest. 'I had quite forgotten—in the excitement!'

'I do not intend to go to university!' she said firmly, her eyes a clear grey on his face, refusing to be intimidated.

'But you said that you were quite excited about it when Alain was here,' he reminded her with raised brows.

'Alain is a stranger and I had no intention of causing an embarrassing scene in front of a stranger!' she said, her head coming up as she continued to face him squarely.

'I see!' He looked at her determined face. 'Let us forget him for a moment and concentrate on you. You are clever, they tell me that you are on the edge of brilliance. The obvious thing for you is to go to university and I can see no common sense in your refusal. You are totally untrained. Do you simply intend to live on your wealth when you are old enough? Have you mapped out a life of the idle rich for yourself?' He sounded really scornful and she sprang to her feet.

'Don't you see? Can't you even try to understand? I have been in a school for the better part of my life! I have never lived! I want to be free!'

He stood too and came over to her, taking her shoulders in his strong hands.

'What will you do, then, with this freedom?'

'I'll get a job!' she said excitedly, relieved that he was not shouting and angry. 'This time, I'll get a really interesting job that I can enjoy. Even if I have to get one after another I will finally get one that is me!'

For a moment he smiled down at her, shaking his head in rueful acceptance as he moved away.

'Very well,' he said softly, 'but not without my approval!' he added, turning back and staring at her firmly.

Beth was delighted and it showed on her face.

'I'll begin at once, tomorrow!'

'No! I will not be here. I do not want you wandering round Paris in any haphazard manner. We will deal with your future properly and methodically.'

In his determination, he gripped her shoulders again, his hands immediately softening as he felt her anxious reaction. 'I shall be away for perhaps two weeks. I am going to Rome and Milan, after that, I shall probably go to Madrid. We are opening a new salon there in the spring and there is quite a lot to arrange.'

'Oh!' Beth's eyes opened wide at this globe-trotting, mentioned so casually, and he looked down at her with softened eyes.

'You would like to come with me, Beth?' he asked quietly. 'I will take you if you want to come.'

For a second, she felt a great wave of excitement, and indecision rose in her expressive eyes but it was quelled as soon as it rose. She would not fly. She would never be able to face that, and the golden hope that Gaetan held out for her had to be refused. For a moment there, she had seen herself in Rome, Milan, Madrid with Gaetan, her friendship with him growing, her nerves relaxing in the warmth and security he made her feel so often, but she managed a brilliant smile of refusal as she delicately disengaged herself from his restraining hands.

She almost longed to be back within the circle of magic that had threatened to grow as he had held her and kissed her, but they were new and alarming feelings and she moved to the door.

'Oh, no, thank you,' she said swiftly. 'I—I don't want to go.'

'Two weeks is not a long time,' he coaxed, 'and I do not really want to leave you alone quite so soon.'

'I've been alone for a long time,' she reminded him quickly, afraid that he would press the point and find out why she did not want to go. 'I'm more than capable of looking after myself. In any case, I'm here in your house. I can hardly starve!' It all came out a little sharply and his expression changed to coolness.

'That is true! I will try not to worry about you, then. Goodnight, Beth. I will see you in approximately two weeks' time.'

He turned away and she bit her lip in vexation. Their sudden and new-found friendship seemed to have drained away so quickly, leaving her quite depressed. She went to bed without another word.

In the morning Gaetan was gone, and after a quick breakfast Beth wandered around exploring the house and grounds. Everything was beautiful, peaceful, with all the signs of wealth that there were in fact about Gaetan himself. It was a little cold, though, for lingering in the garden, and after lunch she made her way to the library, intent upon finding the books that Gaetan had said she might borrow.

It was definitely a room that was his alone. She had not noticed it so much when Alain was there the night before, but now, without distractions, it spoke to her of Gaetan, the very air sang of him, and to her consternation she found that she was missing him badly. It helped little to remind herself that they often fought bitterly; somehow, in this short space of time, he had succeeded in wiping out the months in England when she had been struggling and alone. She was safe!

She curled up in one of the chairs and read, quite startled to find the time passing quickly and bewildered when Madame Benoir showed in a grinning Alain.

'While the cat is away...' he murmured, as Madame Benoir left to bring coffee. 'I could not resist the challenge that you threw out last night, Beth. I thought it a good idea to pounce upon you before you could give any orders to Madame Benoir.'

'But Gaetan is away!' she said quickly, feeling inexpressibly guilty and showing it.

'I *know*,' he laughed. 'If he had not been, I would not have come. I can at least take coffee with you, surely, without your calling to have me thrown out. Louis is so very rough, and quite strong for his age.'

As before, he had her laughing at once, and of course he stayed, but she would not be coaxed into going out; that would be really throwing down the gauntlet to Gaetan, and she was mindful also of what he had said about Alain, 'He is a man and a Frenchman at that!' She refused all offers of a night out.

His coming, though, left her a little restless and she began to ask herself why it was not possible to go out the next day and look for a job. By bedtime, she had convinced herself that it was a good idea. She had not actually made any promise to Gaetan about staying in, and he could hardly expect her to remain in the house for two whole weeks. In the morning, she called a taxi and went into the city to search.

She found, however, that there was about as much work for an unskilled person in Paris as there was in London, and her English accent went very much against her. It did not help either that she was wearing

Vernais clothes, nobody seemed to take her seriously. The general idea seemed to be that she was a very rich young lady at a loose end. Nobody wanted that kind of employee. Even so, she went out every day, looking and enquiring until she was exhausted, too tired at night really to do justice to the dinners that Madame Benoir placed before her. And after only six days, Gaetan returned, unexpectedly and rather violently.

She was in the library. Dressed in new white jeans and a dark blue blouse and with her brightly coloured sandals kicked off and lying beside her, she was sprawled out on the settee reading, having given herself a day off from job-finding, when he stormed into the room.

'Gaetan! You're back!' The unexpectedly violent arrival of her guardian went unnoticed for a second as a great wave of gladness flooded through her. Suddenly the world was alive again, and her frustrations of the past few days fled as if they had never been.

'*Oui!* I am back, *mademoiselle*, and wanting a few explanations!'

It sank in then that he was furious, and she struggled to her knees on the settee, her great grey eyes astonished at his annoyance.

'I—I don't understand, Gaetan,' she stammered worriedly.

'Oh, how innocently said!' he rasped. 'Neither do I understand, *mademoiselle*. I do not understand why you have been entertaining Alain and going off daily to meet him when I expressly warned you of the folly of such actions!'

'But I...' She was going to tell him that it was not true, but his anger scared her. She had also been looking for work when he had expressly forbidden that too.

'You have lost weight while I have been away, and not surprising either!' he ground out. 'Apparently you have been having such a good time that you have been unable to eat your dinner at night and have fallen exhausted into bed!'

'Oh, Madame Benoir has really been busy telling you about me, hasn't she?' said Beth with trembling lips. She felt quite disappointed with Madame Benoir, and her face was downcast.

'She was ordered to care for you and you have made it impossible as you have rarely been in the house! From a very bad attack of a virus, straight to living the life of a . . .!' He seemed suddenly to realise just what he was implying and his eyes stared intently at Beth's red cheeks and quivering lips.

She made no attempt to speak and he turned savagely away, his hands in his pockets as he paced about.

'You had better tell me what happened when you were out with Alain,' he said suddenly in a weary voice, adding tersely, 'He will have some explanations to give too. He is supposed to be working, not trying to lead you astray!'

'I have not been out with Alain, *monsieur*,' she said quietly, too afraid to address him by his first name now.

'He came here!' he rasped, spinning round to face her. 'I do not imagine that he came to see me, knowing as he did that I was in Italy!'

'He came to see me,' she assured him softly, 'but I refused to go out with him.'

'Why?' he asked with dark narrowed eyes. 'I know that he can be very persuasive with the ladies.'

'You warned me, *monsieur*, and I did not forget it,' Beth said, blushing even more deeply when she recalled exactly how she had been warned.

'So where exactly have you been then, *mademoiselle*?' he asked with an intrigued and suspicious look at her, coming to the settee where she still knelt and taking her two wrists in his hand.

'I—I went to look for work, for a job,' she said very quickly, before her courage finally gave out.

'You have been roaming the streets of Paris, alone?' he murmured with a deep and menacing quiet. 'You have openly disregarded my express wishes that you did not fail to understand, and you have been wandering about looking for work like a poor and uncared-for little waif?'

When she did not answer his grip tightened even further and he went on relentlessly.

'So what work did you find then, *mademoiselle*? Are you now a waitress in a cocktail bar, a clerk on the railways, a fish porter?' He was horribly sarcastic, and her eyes filled with tears of anger as she glared at him.

'I'm nothing! I'm still what I was before, utterly at your mercy!' He didn't look too pitying.

'Ah, they would not give you a job, *mademoiselle*? They said that you did not have sufficient experience to be a fish porter or a railway clerk?'

She snatched her hands away from him and struggled to her feet, facing him furiously, tears rolling down her cheeks.

'I was too well dressed!' she stormed angrily. 'They looked at those damned expensive clothes and thought I was simply amusing myself!'

For a second he looked startled and then he sat down; he actually had to sit down to laugh, he was laughing so much!

She fled from the room and raced upstairs to her bedroom, furiously angry and disappointed. She had been glad to see him, actually glad! He was hateful!

He was like a monstrous Victorian older brother! There was not one spark of kindness in his whole body.

Gaetan came in without knocking as she stood staring out of the window, her eyes so filled with tears that she saw nothing.

'I am sorry, Beth,' he said quietly when he saw how upset she was. 'I have a very bad temper, and although it is not an excuse for my rudeness, please believe that I was horrified at the idea that you had been in any danger.'

'I believe you,' she sniffed, wiping her tears away with the back of her hand and not turning. 'Now will you please go away.'

'No.' He was right behind her without her knowing and he turned her unwilling body to face him. 'I will not go and leave you so unhappy.'

'I'm not unhappy. I'm angry!' she said with an attempt at defiance that did not fool him at all.

He cupped her chin with his hand, his other arm tightening around her.

'My poor little Beth,' he murmured softly. 'I am a brute, forgive me.' His dark eyes were intent on her face as she opened her eyes unwillingly to look at him, startled by the warmth of his voice.

'I haven't been seeing Alain,' she assured him quietly, her voice rising in protest as she added, 'I couldn't stay in for two whole weeks by myself. You— you weren't there!'

'I am here now,' he said softly. 'I gave up my trip to Madrid.'

'Why?' she whispered, her eyes wide and a little worried.

'You were alone. I did not want that. I came back.'

He watched her silently, his eyes on her trembling lips, and all her unhappiness began to ease away.

'If you will allow me, *mademoiselle*,' he said with a smile, 'I would be honoured to take you out to lunch.'

'Now?' She looked at him in a happy daze, her eyes still wet with tears.

'It is lunch time,' he assured her quietly. 'You may change or come as you are, if you will consent to accompany me.'

She was suddenly so happy, so secure that she threw her arms around his waist and hugged him.

'Oh! I would love to, Gaetan!'

He carefully extricated himself and for a second she thought that he was annoyed. He smiled down at her, though, as he moved away.

'Ah! I have not forgotten that you have disobeyed me, little minx,' he said quietly. 'You will not wind me around your little finger. I will be ready in fifteen minutes,' he added as he walked from the room.

Beth watched him with a kind of breathless wonder inside her. She had no doubts at all that she could not wind him around her finger but he seemed to be able to do that to her.

The luncheon date lasted all day, as it turned out. With the protective cloak of Gaetan's kindness once more around her she was relaxed with him, and he seemed happy to talk to her about his trip, telling her about Rome and Milan, places she had never visited, so that it was a very lengthy luncheon.

Afterwards, they roamed through the unfashionable parts of the city, Beth's hand tucked into Gaetan's arm as she drank in the life and movement, the vivacity of the Parisians. They watched the lights on the river, leaning over bridges to see the boats go by, and then wandered into unexpected little squares and up endless flights of steps that lifted them to see the city from a different angle.

It was quite late when they stopped for dinner at a small café and Beth felt more contented than she had ever before felt in her life, quite prepared to sit in the peace of the sudden silence that had come over Gaetan.

'I do not wish to spoil our beautiful evening, Beth,' he said quietly, making her colour flare when she heard that he too had thought it beautiful, 'but there is something that we really must discuss if today's angry scene is not to be repeated.' He sat looking at her steadily, his coffee cradled in his long fingers as he chose his words with care. 'I do not wish to cut you off from the rest of the world, but even if you are almost twenty, you are very young because of your life, because of the way you have been forced to live. It is useless to tell me that other people are in the same position and are on their own in the world; I cannot seek them out and correct the world for them. You, though, are my responsibility; I must and I do care for you.'

'I'm sorry that I worried you,' she began but he put his cup down and covered her hand with his.

'I am not wanting apologies,' he said quietly, 'only understanding. I do not wish to deny you the realisation of the sweetness and the bitterness of life, it is this that makes us as we are, but I must protect you. Give up this idea of work, Beth. Consider the university. Spend your time studying and then enjoying yourself in safety, and by the time the September intake of students is due, you may feel very differently. I will not deny you your freedom. I only wish that you temper it with caution.'

When he spoke like that, she would do anything for him, she realised, and she also knew the heavy burden of responsibility that he bore.

'Can I agree without actually making a promise?' she enquired with such caution that he laughed, his white teeth gleaming against his tanned face.

'Yes. We have a bargain?' he enquired. 'A trial period?'

'All right!' She looked up and smiled at him enchantingly and his face clouded a little.

'Oh, Beth!' he said softly as if it really hurt. 'You are so heartbreakingly young.'

'I age really fast when you shout at me,' she assured him with a little grin and he smiled again, his moment of sadness passing.

'Perhaps,' he said thoughtfully, 'you should after all consider the possibility of allowing Alain to escort you from time to time.'

'I'd rather be with you!' Beth said quickly, speaking without thinking. She had a sudden feeling of loss, a quick flicker of fear in the pit of her stomach that was nothing to do with his original warnings when she had met Alain.

'Alain is quite safe to be with,' he said quietly. 'If I were not absolutely sure of that, then I would not have suggested it.'

'But you said...'

'I remember. It was a general warning only and also,' he paused, looking a little rueful, 'also your appearance as a young woman instead of an angry teenager quite startled me. Alain's immediate reaction to you also made me a little too protective, perhaps.'

'Do you want me to go out with Alain, then?' she murmured in a dull voice, and his hand covered hers again.

'I said, perhaps we should consider it, notice the word—perhaps.'

'You want me to be safe,' she reminded him in a hurried voice. 'I'll be safest with you.'

'I am a man too, Beth,' he said softly, his eyes on her delicate and beautiful face. 'It is my duty, my pleasure and my good fortune to be also your protector. Let us leave the subject, shall we? Tomorrow I will take you to see the place where I work.'

In the morning she was once more with Gaetan, sitting beside him in his fast red sports car as it slid in and out of the alarming traffic, on her way for the first time to see where he worked.

Madeleine had already told her that designers normally called their place of work a warehouse, so she had a vague idea of what to expect. Even if she had not, Gaetan was particularly silent this morning, so she knew that there would be little information coming from him. In fact she was really surprised that he had brought her at all. He seemed to be in a mood.

The building was three-storeyed, surrounded by a security fence that would have done justice to any secret defence project, and at her mention of this, Gaetan assured her that security was a very necessary part of their everyday life.

'There are three collections a year,' he told her seriously. 'A preview of them would be worth a fortune to our competitors. You will have to realise that anything you see here is not to be spoken of outside the house or the works.'

'I don't have anyone to speak to,' Beth said, meaning it to be a light remark. 'There is you, Madame Benoir and Louis and then there is Madeleine. Since they are obviously to be trusted, who else is there?'

'I realise that there is little in your life at the moment,' he said, a trifle sharply, 'but if you can be patient you will find that things will happen. A new life cannot be built within a few days.'

It was unfair, especially as she had not been complaining at all, but she knew that he was in a mood for some reason so she kept quiet, making no attempt to explain.

'I see no reason for you to be miserable and depressed about things!' he said sharply as he heard her deep sigh. 'I am not keeping you a prisoner, nor am I about to sell you into slavery!' The gates opened at his imperious blast on the horn and he drove into a courtyard at the back of the building.

Beth wasn't listening any more. Her eyes had been scanning the high building and her heartbeats had quickened at the sight of the sheer wall that fell to the cobbled courtyard. Set high in the wall were huge loading-doors, a relic of the place's history. They were now closed, but they were there, and her active imagination visualised the drop from those huge doors to the cobbled yard beneath. She could see in her mind's eye men leaning from there in the days when this building had really been a warehouse, and the nearby river had been used to transport the goods that had been stored here long ago. She closed her eyes in fear, a fear that she never spoke of, turning her suddenly white face away so that Gaetan would not see her reaction to this height.

He was, as usual, too quick for her and his hand came to her face at once, turning her back to him.

'What is the matter?' he asked, looking at her intently. 'Are you afraid to meet the people here? There is nothing to be afraid of. You are with me.'

'I am not afraid, *monsieur*,' she said stiffly, fighting down her real fear. 'If I don't like them I can always ignore them.'

'You were not at all indifferent to Alain when he called at the house,' he said with narrowed eyes. 'He will be here today, so there is one person at least that you will like.'

'I was merely being polite,' she said, trying to hang her head and failing miserably because of his restraining hand. 'Anyway, you were there.'

'And what is that supposed to mean?' he asked impatiently.

'I—well—I feel safe with you,' she explained, greatly subdued by his harsh voice and the determined hand on her face. She risked a look at him and found that he was smiling, a very mocking smile that worried her.

'There are plenty of people who would not share your trust in me,' he murmured, his eyes touching her face and hair with slashing intensity. 'It assures me of your extreme youth.'

'You—you're not old, so why do you speak like that?' she said softly, a little shaky now.

'I am old enough to know better,' he said with a sardonic smile. 'I keep remembering that and, one word of warning, do not do anything to get Alain into trouble. He is scared of me as it is.'

'I know how he feels,' Beth muttered and his dark brow lifted arrogantly.

'Indeed? I do not recall giving you reason to be afraid of me. You are often ready to fight me, and you have little control over your sharp tongue.'

'You've deliberately picked a quarrel with me!' said Beth with a great deal of reproof in her voice. 'You've done it so that I'll be too scared to talk to Alain!'

'You have a wild imagination,' he said bitingly, getting out of the car and coming to help her out. 'However, perhaps you could manage to give the impression when we are here among strangers that you are happy in my company. You may shiver when we are alone.'

He was towering over her as he helped her out, and suddenly he was smiling.

'Courage, ma petite,' he advised softly, his hand on the nape of her neck soothing, melting her inside. *'Tout va bien.'*

'It is not!' she said accusingly. 'Not when you're angry for nothing at all.'

'But I am not angry, *ma chère*! Come!' He took her hand and led her to the building, merely smiling at her rather tragic sigh. He was very often quite impossible, she decided.

The impression of wealth and elegance was there as soon as they entered the building. The ground floor was very clearly occupied by offices and showrooms where clients would be welcomed graciously, but Gaetan merely strode through to the stairs, ignoring the lift, nodding casually to people who sprang to their feet at the sight of him, people who tried hard not to look too closely at the delicately beautiful girl who appeared to be clinging to his hand. In actual fact, it was Gaetan who held Beth fast, almost racing her along.

As they progressed upwards Beth looked round her with interest. There was activity in every room, huge drawing-boards on tables, people carrying fabulous rolls of cloth. There was noise, activity, a driving energy and bewildering movement, and time after time Gaetan was stopped and asked for advice. Sometimes he would be called across the huge rooms and then Beth was left standing by the door, her eyes taking in all the activity and avoiding the admiring glances that came her way.

Their progress was slow now, but always he watched her. Whatever happened, she could be assured that, looking up, she would find Gaetan's eyes on her every few minutes, their dark depths all-seeing, noticing her growing interest and not missing either the looks that came her way.

By the time they came to the top floor, Beth had the distinct feeling that she was being led to some sort of sacrifice, and her hand tightened involuntarily in his, making him glance at her quickly and murmur in amusement, 'Stop worrying. I guarantee that when we leave here, you will be with me.'

'Are you going to force me on to Alain, *monsieur*?' she enquired, huskily suspicious.

'*Ma foi*! I am not! I said that we would consider him, but I also said perhaps—and that in the distant future!'

'I remember that you were pleased when I refused to go out with him,' she said looking up into his dark face with shimmering grey eyes. 'Now you seem to have changed your mind.'

'Perhaps then I did not realise how...' He stopped in the darkened hallway before the doors of the last room at the top of the building. 'Anything at all that I do for you will be for your own good, Beth,' he said firmly. 'Please try to co-operate.'

'Just how far will I be expected to co-operate when I finally go out with Alain?' she said pertly, determined for some reason to shake him out of his aloof mood.

'Do not try your hand at living dangerously, *petite*,' he said threateningly, his voice deadly soft. 'Not with me! I would not wish any man who escorts you to have too much enjoyment, not if he wishes to survive the experience!'

She blushed at the obvious innuendo and dropped her eyes, regretting her rash remarks, but her face was tilted upwards at once and his dark eyes roamed over her hot cheeks.

'Be good,' he advised. 'And do not call me *monsieur*!' He bent swiftly and dropped a kiss on her startled lips, a curious kiss that seemed to taste her, and she was being led inside before she could even begin to recover from the shock of it.

CHAPTER FIVE

THE place was a beehive of activity, obviously the hub of everything, and though the heavy swing doors cut it off from the stairs Beth could see that the whole of the top floor was one huge room. Gaetan motioned her ahead of him, releasing her hand now and taking her arm in a firm grip that was both comforting and threatening, and she was not sure where her breathlessness came from. Perhaps she was too scared to breathe deeply, but somehow she thought that it was the kiss that had left her feeling so weak.

It had been a mere brush of his lips on hers, but the effect had been frightening in the intensity of feeling that had shot through her so unexpectedly, and she was left feeling quite incapable of facing strangers, dreading the time when Gaetan would be called away from her side and his hand would no longer be holding her arm.

She need not have worried, because he did not appear to have the slightest intention of letting her go, and here everyone seemed too involved in their work even to notice her.

'Gaetan! What a time to arrive! We've been waiting! Everything is held up!' The accusing voice had Beth looking round as a slim, dark-haired woman bore down on them. She was attractive and she wore the most enormous spectacles that Beth had ever seen, Beth waited for Gaetan to growl at her for the angry tone. He did not, however.

'You know that I have other duties now,' he said quite mildly. 'There is Beth to look after. Being a guardian is a little time-consuming.'

Beth cringed at the tone. She might have been no more than ten years old the way he spoke of her, and her face tightened perceptibly as she glared at him.

'The collection is nowhere near finished!' the woman said worriedly. 'I can't promise anything if you don't appear when I expect you to be there.'

'If the boss can't take time off, who can?' Gaetan murmured in amusement, getting a dragon-like snort from his accuser. 'Meet Beth. You'll be seeing plenty of her and she is my excuse.'

'She's beautiful.' The angry face dissolved into an attractive smile and Beth found her hand being shaken with genuine pleasure. 'She's no excuse, though. She's a grown woman and well able to take care of herself, so don't go looking for a way out there.'

'Perhaps I had better tell you, Beth, this is Marie-Annette who runs everything and attempts to bully me.' Gaetan looked down at Beth and smiled wickedly. 'As you are a woman you can protect me from her.' He looked very doubtful, and Beth wasn't sure either if she liked the gleaming amusement in his dark eyes as he looked at her mockingly. To him she was not in any way a woman.

There was no chance to reply, however, because another woman had come from the end of the room and threw herself into his arms, almost knocking Beth off her feet.

'Gaetan! I expected to see you yesterday. I've been so worried. You know that I should have been with you as usual!'

'It was not necessary,' Gaetan replied, a sort of amused indulgence on his face. Beth thought that he probably did not like this display of affection in front of everyone here, but he did not stiffen up as far as Beth could tell. He gently disengaged himself from the clinging arms that seemed to wish to choke him but he smiled down at the woman.

'All that I have to know again I have taped for you, Gabrielle. You can get it down in black and white this afternoon and that will be all that is necessary.'

The girl seemed to notice Beth for the first time, but Beth was not in any way deceived. There was a whole lot of play-acting going on here, and the dark eyes that turned on her were gleaming with a barely hidden anger.

'I see that you have someone with you,' she said archly. 'Does this mean that I am to be discarded, *chéri*?'

'Allow me to introduce Mademoiselle Elizabeth Craig,' Gaetan said with a quick and ironical look at Beth's stunned face. No doubt he was quite accustomed to having women fight over him, Beth thought angrily, noticing that the French girl did not hold out her hand in greeting. 'I feel, *ma chère*, that you will be somewhat neglected. Beth will take up a great deal of my time for the next few months.'

Beth's grey eyes flashed angrily to meet his dark and sardonic gaze, but at this moment Marie-Annette chose to intervene with a waspishness she had not shown at all to Beth.

'She is so beautiful, don't you think, Gabrielle? With a little more height she would outshine all our models. That glorious hair and that lovely skin. The English women are so lucky.'

The answer came from Gaetan which was as well, Beth thought, because it was clear that Gabrielle was not about to add anything to this small hymn of praise.

'You may forget any ideas you have in that direction, Marie-Annette,' he said firmly, his lips tightening at the mere suggestion of it. 'She stays firmly and securely with me. Being wealthy in her own right, she does not need to earn her living and, in any case, she has too much to do.'

'Looking after you, *chéri*?' Gabrielle asked, her amusement a thin veil covering anger.

'You must come here and see how we work, Beth,' Marie-Annette interrupted with a smile that was all feline battle. Her eyes were really on Gabrielle.

'You will meet her again, no doubt,' Gaetan assured her tightly. 'I do not intend to let her stray too far from under my wing.'

The comforting protection of his words suddenly seemed a little like a set of steel bars, but fortunately Gabrielle chose to change the subject. Whether she was relieved to find that Beth was merely Gaetan's ward or whether she too saw the signals of danger in Gaetan's unsmiling face Beth did not know, but she was quite suddenly all sweetness and light, her dark eyes smiling at Gaetan, ignoring Beth as she had done at the first meeting.

'When did you get back then, Gaetan?' she asked, looking up at him with a warm smile.

'Yesterday lunch time,' he told her shortly. 'I was too busy to call into the works and I shall no doubt be busy for the rest of the day.'

'If there was anything to do then why did you not call me?' Gabrielle asked plaintively, her face flushed with pleasure when Gaetan said,

'There was nothing to do, *chérie*.' His added words, however, drove the smile from her face. 'I will give you the tape to get typed up. I came home and took Beth out at once. We were out until very late in fact.

And now, Marie-Annette, if you are to pressurise me let us get on with it. The rest of my day is Beth's.'

He marched Beth off down the room, close on the heels of Marie-Annette, leaving Gabrielle to stare angrily after them, and Beth went stiffly and tightly, clearly an unwilling captive.

'Relax! Stop worrying so much!' Gaetan said softly but emphatically as they moved amongst the hectic activity of the workroom. 'Nobody is about to bite you.'

'Except perhaps Gabrielle!' Beth hissed in an equally low but emphatic voice. 'I did not expect to be used as a means of making your girlfriend jealous!'

'Gabrielle Dubois is my Personal Assistant!' Gaetan bit out, but to his great and obvious surprise Beth did not allow him to go any further.

'However personal she is has nothing whatever to do with me, *monsieur*!' she muttered angrily. 'I do not like, though, to be used as a means to further your amorous interests!'

'Amorous! You know the meaning of the word then?' he grated quickly. 'I think that it will be better if you concentrate on your own affairs, *mademoiselle*, and leave mine to me!'

'Just as long as I am to get the opportunity, *monsieur*!' she snapped and, seeing Alain, who turned and caught sight of her, his face lighting up with pleasure, she pulled away from Gaetan's restraining hand and made her way across to Alain with as good an imitation of Gabrielle Dubois' greeting of her guardian as she could muster without the actual physical assault. Thereafter she stayed firmly with Alain, glancing defiantly at Gaetan every time his eyes flashed to her, an occurrence that was frequent and his gaze said but one thing—wait until we are alone, *mademoiselle*!

By the time they were ready to leave, however, his anger appeared to have changed to indifference, and he hardly spoke at all, even when they stopped for a late lunch on the way back to the house.

'I think that for the rest of the afternoon you should get a little fresh air,' he said moodily as they drove out of the city.

'I agree,' Beth said coldly, battling with many feelings. She admitted that she was disappointed in him, at the way he had used her to arouse jealousy in Gabrielle Dubois. The girl would not have dared to behave like that with someone like Gaetan Vernais if she was not on the most intimate terms with him, and the very idea sent waves of bitterness through Beth for a reason she hadn't yet succeeded in fathoming.

She was annoyed with herself too. She had begun to set him up on a pedestal, almost without realising it, and that was simply foolish. He was much too virile and masculine to be anything but what he clearly was. It was nothing to her how many hearts he broke, and she was not about to let him intrude into her life and upset her plans.

Already, things were not as she would have wished, not at all what she had imagined. He had insisted that she change her appearance, and with the change had come for her a change in personality. She gave thought now to how she looked, to her clothes, and to how Gaetan reacted to her. It was annoying and time-consuming and she found herself blaming everything on him, especially this business of Alain.

She regretted her too-hasty action in going to Alain. She had got herself into a situation that would have to be played through to the end, at least for today.

'Tonight, I will take you out,' he said quietly, clearly battling with his own rising annoyance, but Beth did not look across at him.

'I'm sorry, *monsieur*,' she said politely. 'I have already been invited out this evening and I have accepted!'

'Alain?' he grated, shooting a glance across at her with dark and glittering eyes.

'Naturally! You did say that it was to be considered. I hope, *monsieur*, that the arrangement is to your liking?'

'Don't be so damned irritating!' he suddenly snarled, bringing the car to a grinding halt at the side of the leafy road. 'You have done this to annoy me and you have certainly succeeded! I told you that Alain was to be considered only, and that in the future. I did not expect that you would throw yourself at him immediately!'

'I did not throw myself at him!' Beth snapped in annoyance. 'Mademoiselle Dubois threw herself at you! I greeted Alain in a civilised manner, was invited out and accepted!'

'Gabrielle is over-excitable,' Gaetan muttered angrily, his eyes roaming over her face with moody annoyance. 'The people there know her. You were unprepared, that's all.'

'I shall never be prepared for little scenes like that, no matter how well you train me, *monsieur*!' Beth rejoined tartly, her face flushing under his intent scrutiny. 'As to Alain, I have merely brought the time forward, decided for myself. Clearly you will be too occupied in the evenings to escort me!'

'*Ma foi!* You sound as cold as ice and as hard as nails and I know that you are neither! What is eating you, eh? Gabrielle is my Personal Assistant. She was once a model and she knows the business inside out. I would not like to be without her. Naturally also, I take her out in the evenings.'

'It has nothing to do with me, *monsieur*,' Beth said coolly. 'As to my own arrangements, Alain will collect me at seven-thirty and take me out to dinner and to a show.'

'Just so that he remembers that you are my responsibility,' he said darkly. 'See to it that dinner and a show is all that he enjoys!'

'No harm can come to a—child, *monsieur*!' Beth said sarcastically, wishing the words back as soon as they had left her mouth, because he stopped frowning.

'Ah!' he murmured thoughtfully. He looked at her for a moment and then added, 'I think, *petite*, that you may not have enough mirrors in your room or perhaps you do not look at yourself often enough. It is quite true, what Marie-Annette said, you would make a stunning model, so very unusual and beautiful.' He ran his hand gently over her face, his eyes moodily intent. 'The English skin is really astonishingly soft and clear. It must be your damp and dismal climate.'

Beth sat stunned and mesmerised under this unexpected change of tactics and his hand stayed compellingly on her hot cheek, his eyes glittering dark on her face.

Her eyes moved to the sensuous lure of his lips, remembering her reaction when he had kissed her, and for a second he was completely still, his head close to hers.

'It is perhaps a good idea,' he said in an almost dazed voice. 'Take care, though, when you are with Alain.'

Beth nodded but it was very clear that neither of them was paying much thought to Alain. Unknowingly, her lips parted invitingly, and with a movement that was almost anger, he grasped her arms and moved her forward.

His head came down slowly and she had plenty of time to escape, but she did not even try. It was like tasting forbidden fruit, tempting the devil, a wild and almost wicked desire to feel again the surge of heat through her body, and it happened as she had known that it would.

The kiss was gentle, almost tender, suddenly deepening and then withdrawing in a tantalising movement that almost made her cry out in frustration. She kept her eyes closed and he lifted his head, his hand still beneath the heavy fall of her hair, cradling her head, and when she opened her eyes he was looking at her with the same moody expression on his dark, handsome face.

'Why—why did you do that?' she whispered in a shaky voice, her eyes wide and appealing.

'Perhaps I could not resist the invitation!' he said harshly, moving abruptly from her. 'In France we do not make quite so much of a friendly kiss as is made in England.' He shot a dark and angry glance at her. 'Do not continue to call me *monsieur*,' he advised in a threatening voice, 'or I may decide to take a little kiss somewhat further and propel your education into another stage entirely.'

'You're not civilised!' Beth managed to get out in a frightened voice. 'I sincerely hope that Alain is more civilised than this!'

'*Mais certainement!*' He suddenly laughed, turning away and starting the car. 'He will be watching his step, I assure you. He is not your guardian and he knows very well who is!'

'I—I'll stay in if you like,' Beth offered, suddenly very subdued, but her offer gained her a slanting look of amusement and a definite shake of the head.

'And sit at my feet as I nod before the fire? No thank you, *ma chère*! Now that you are off my hands for the evening, I am free to go out and enjoy myself. I was not too happy about disappointing Gabrielle, she expects to be taken out often. Remind me to give you a key before you go. Madame Benoir will be in her room with her television and deaf to the world. I will not be in until the early hours.'

Going out with Alain became a regular part of Beth's life during the next few weeks. There was rarely a day when he did not call her and arrange some trip or outing for the evening, and she found his company soothing after the rather alarming presence of Gaetan.

Apparently satisfied that she was quite safe with Alain, Gaetan seemed to be content to leave her to herself, and she spent much of her time indoors studying, finding it quite absorbing after her long spell away from any intellectual activity.

She fitted into her new life with a readiness that showed in her growing self-confidence. She gained a few much-needed pounds in weight, her skin took on a delicate tan and all in all her life was a daily pleasure, her satisfaction with it showing on her face.

There was only one nagging thing to unsettle her and that was Gaetan himself. Having handed her over, as it were, to Alain, he now rarely saw her. They met at mealtimes, but as likely as not they were both out in the evening and Gaetan himself seemed to be snowed under with work, preoccupied and distant, so that when he did make his presence felt she was invariably taken by surprise and thrown back into the small whirl of internal panic that nearness to him was beginning to increase with every day she saw him.

'I trust neither you nor Alain have made any arrangements for tonight?' Gaetan said briefly one morning as he prepared to leave for the city.

'Well—no, as a matter of fact we haven't,' Beth said quietly, her face suddenly wary as Gaetan paused on his way out to look down at her steadily.

'Good, I half expected him to have forgotten about tonight in his great enthusiasm for your company. You are both on duty tonight.'

'How do you mean?' Beth asked anxiously, her eyes widening as his hand tilted her face and he smiled down at her with his usual sardonic expression.

'Nothing too alarming. There is a fashion show that we are to attend. Nothing special, but it is always a good idea to take a look at the opposition. In any case, we are invited and it would be the height of bad taste to be absent. Alain does know about it. We will be leaving about seven-thirty. There is a dinner and then the showing. Later I expect there will be some event or other, but we can leave after the showing if you are too bored.'

'Oh! I'm sure I won't be!' Beth was unaware of the eagerness on her face and a smile twitched at his lips as he noticed the glow in her eyes.

'Ah! You have developed a taste for the finer things of life? I must see to it that you are taken again to the salon, perhaps next week.'

'I've got plenty of clothes,' she protested quietly, but the hand on her chin stayed firm and steady as he smiled down at her.

'A woman can never have too many clothes, surely?' he laughed. 'When that time comes I shall be out of business. In any case, you are a very good advertisement for the firm. When we have got the next collection out of the way I shall design some things especially for you.'

He moved his hand from her face with a slow caressing movement that she knew was accidental but it brought the colour rushing up under her lightly tanned skin.

'You will need a very nice evening gown for to-night,' he remarked quietly. 'If you do not have one, ring Madeleine and go out for one this morning. Only a Vernais of course,' he added with a teasing threat in his voice as his hand suddenly swept over her golden hair.

He left the house and Beth found that she was smiling like a simpleton, her heart beating fast and furiously, and all because he had gone back to his kindly teasing ways. She was not in any doubt either as to why she was so happy about tonight. It was not the clothes, she was looking forward to seeing more of Gaetan, to dressing up and gaining his approval, it added a glow to her day that simply refused to go.

It was still there when she was carefully tucked into the Rolls-Royce by Gaetan at seven that evening on their way to pick up Alain, and the blush that had coloured her face when she had come downstairs to find him waiting, resplendent and wickedly handsome in his white dinner-jacket, his dark eyes running over her with open admiration, was still there.

'*Dieu!* Did I say that I would design something for you? It seems that everything I have designed has been with you in mind even when I had never seen you.' His eyes held her there on the bottom step of the stairs and she waited with her breathing shallow and uneven as he walked slowly forward to take her arm.

The dress was wild silk, a kind of golden pink that brought beautiful colour to her face and contrasted wonderfully with her hair. Tonight she had worn the hairpiece that she had brought back when her hair had been cut. It was a daring thing for her, and at the last minute she had been forced to call in a panic to Madame Benoir who had come in and fixed her hair beautifully, piling it on top of her head in a way that was both sophisticated and youthful, turning the dress into a dreamlike vision of a ball gown of days long passed.

'You will need jewellery,' Gaetan said quietly, his eyes touching her delicate and golden skin, glancing along her smooth and slender shoulders left un-adorned by the low off-the-shoulder dress. She seemed to begin burning as he looked at her and for a moment their eyes met and held, an unreadable message in Gaetan's that was quickly hidden as he led her to the library door.

Now, sitting next to him in the gathering dusk of the evening, a string of milky pearls around her neck, Beth felt the nearest thing to complete happiness that she had ever felt in her life. Tonight there was a new warmth to Gaetan, and though she still had no idea whether or not he admitted to her being a woman, he was certainly proud of her, and for now it was all she needed.

Alain too was all praise as he slid easily into the back of the car when they called for him, his eyes on Beth with an adoring pleasure.

'I thought that Gabrielle would be here tonight,' he said as the car moved off heading further into Paris.

'She will meet us there and return with us later,' Gaetan explained, and Beth's new-found happiness fled as swiftly as it had come as understanding dawned. She was not with Gaetan, she was with Alain. Gabrielle was to be with Gaetan and only the fact that she lived in Gaetan's house had led to his bringing her at all.

As if he felt her change of mood with no word spoken, Gaetan glanced at her and then as quickly looked away, and when she dared a quick look in his direction she saw that his face was no longer warm and smiling, his hard jaw was set and determined, his face bleak and coldly handsome.

Beth was thankful for her many outings with Alain as they settled into their places for the dinner that was to open the proceedings. There was a glitter here that a few weeks ago would have had her in a wild panic. It was an event that brought forth fashion designers and the glamorous ladies who wore their clothes, and she knew that when the show began there would be some of the best and most beautiful models in the country showing the clothes to the very knowledgeable people who were gathered there.

By now she had been several times to Gaetan's warehouse and had seen the elegant models who were there to show off the clothes to clients and to be on call when needed, and their glamour had always made her feel uneasy, although Marie-Annette very often treated them impatiently, turning them round like so many beautiful dress props as she pinned material on them and ripped it off again, intent only on her work.

Beth liked her, but she would never like Gabrielle. It was easy to see that Gabrielle had once been a successful model. Her movements were studied and smooth, her make-up perfect and her clothes chic and excellent. She watched Beth almost constantly until it was with relief that Beth was able to turn from the table and watch the show, letting her mind ease up from the constant battering of eyes filled with malice.

It was exciting nevertheless to be in Gaetan's world, and the clothes were lovely, the music and the movement perfectly balanced.

'Well? What do you think, Beth?' Gaetan leaned over her as she sat gazing fixedly at the platform, his breath warm against her skin as he moved closer from his position just behind her.

'Oh! They're beautiful!' She spun round to answer and found to her dismay that his face was merely inches from hers.

'How can they be? I did not design them!' he demanded, smiling into her eyes. 'Whose side are you on anyway, *mademoiselle*?'

'I—I'm always on your side,' she said quietly, looking quickly away, and his soft laughter ran like a warm trickle of liquid down the length of her spine, the small and intimate moment not going unnoticed by Gabrielle, whose eyes instantly narrowed into unbridled annoyance.

There was dancing later and Alain was determined that she should be his partner even if Gaetan had brought her, so she was spared further looks of annoyance from Gabrielle and managed to remain quite calm until they left soon after eleven.

This time too she was placed in the back of the car with Alain, an adroit manoeuvre carried out under Gaetan's nose by both Alain and Gabrielle, for once in accord, and Alain set out to be his usual charming self at once, using the darkness of the car as an excuse to take her hand possessively and talk to her to the exclusion of the others. It suited her well enough, because she had no doubt about her place in the general scheme of things. Gaetan's silence and Gabrielle's assured movements beside him left her in no doubt that she was a small and slightly annoying intrusion into the normal lives that they all led in the glamorous city.

She forced herself into animated conversation that tired her more than the rest of the evening had done, and she was greatly relieved when Alain was dropped off at his home and she was able to sit back in the darkness and relax.

She must have relaxed more than she had intended, because the next thing she knew was that Gaetan was standing by the open window, the cool night air making her shiver, and he had said something, she wasn't at all aware of what.

'I—I'm sorry,' she said, bewildered for a moment to find that they were alone.

'I said, get into the front,' he repeated, reaching inside and taking her hand.

'But where's Gabrielle?' She struggled out, hampered by her wide flowing skirts, and he steadied her for a minute as she swayed tiredly.

'Gabrielle is indoors. I have just dropped her off.' He motioned towards a house set back off the road and she saw that they were still parked half inside the drive.

'Oh, I thought she would be coming back with us.' She turned to close the door but he was there before her, taking her arm then and leading her forward to the passenger door at the front of the car.

'I really cannot think why you should imagine that,' he said in a cool voice. 'I cannot think either why you chose to sit in the back in the first place. As you came here sitting beside me, surely I could have expected to have your company on the return journey.'

'But Gabrielle was there!' She looked at him, astonished, and he grunted irritably, almost pushing her into the car and gathering her skirts in behind her.

'Let us get one thing quite straight,' he rasped as he got in and started the engine, 'Gabrielle is my Personal Assistant, and a frequent companion. She does not own me! Her ways may be odd to you but she knows her job thoroughly and is very useful to me.'

'I really don't know why you're so angry about it all,' Beth said in bewilderment. 'Anyway, Alain wanted to talk to me so it was easier to sit in the back.'

'He talked to you so much that apparently he exhausted you,' Gaetan offered drily. 'Of course, he cannot be expected to know your ways as well as I do, nor your ability to curl up and sleep like a dormouse whenever the chance arises.'

'I don't!' she protested, feeling most unglamorous.

'Yes, you do. I have noticed it many times when you did not even know that I was there. You simply curl into a soft ball and sleep instantly. I have often walked into the library at home and found you sleeping quite delightfully, your books on the floor with your sandals. You have never even known that I have been there.'

'I use up a lot of emotion,' Beth offered uneasily and he glanced at her quickly and keenly.

'What did you use it up on tonight? Alain or the dresses?'

'I—I was just tired,' she murmured, and when she glanced across at him he was smiling that odd and worrying smile, his eyes fixed on the dark ribbon of road before them.

'I can't think why you bothered to get me up and make me sit here,' she said resentfully into the silence. Clearly he had no intention of speaking to her.

'Perhaps I am lonely,' he bantered, 'and in any case, with you beside me I can make quite sure that you do not roll off on to the floor. It is not so easy to curl up here. You are very grumpy now that you have been roused from your little sleep.'

Beth sighed in exasperation. She was either a child or a little furry ball likely to roll up on the floor. What point was there in trying to be glamorous? He might just as well keep his dresses for someone with what he considered to be maturity. She gave a little sniff of annoyance, glaring at him when he began to laugh quietly, determined to walk straight upstairs as soon as they got home.

And that was exactly what she did, except that the effect was rather spoiled by the fact that she had forgotten about the pearls and had to turn and walk back to him as he stood grinning at her from the doorway of the library.

'I have offended further?' he asked with mock alarm.

'I forgot the pearls,' she snapped irritably, avoiding his eyes.

'Ah, yes,' he murmured. 'Come in here. I will put them back into the safe.' She was led into the softly lit room before she could protest and before she could get the pearls off, his hands were warm on her nape as he unfastened them himself, sliding them gently from her skin and placing them on the desk.

'How very lucky they are to have spent the evening around your neck,' he said softly, his eyes crinkling in amused appraisal at her quick blush, his hand detaining her as she turned to hurry from this amusing torture. 'Wait,' he said quietly. 'I am sorry that I have teased you and made you angry. Goodnight, Beth.'

His hands cupped her face gently as he bent to kiss her cheek, a kiss that he would have given to a child, and something inside Beth seemed to snap. She was tired of trying to please him, tired of his mocking tone, his amused laughter, and deep down inside she admitted that she was jealous of the easy hold that Gabrielle Dubois seemed to have on him.

Why should she continue to suffer these small and teasing kisses when not long ago, while she had slept, he had no doubt kissed Gabrielle most thoroughly as if she were a real woman and not a child? She wound her arms round his neck, turning her mouth to his, and deepened the kiss herself, nothing but instinct to guide her as she moved closer, offering her soft lips like a gift.

He was startled, she could tell that. A shudder ran right through him and she realised her mistake as fire shot through her own veins, her angry act backfiring on her as she seemed to burst into flame.

'Oh!' A little cry of panic left her lips as he lifted his head and looked down at her with glittering intensity and she belatedly started to back away, afraid of the feelings she had aroused in herself, afraid of the tightness of his face and the blaze in his eyes.

His arms tightened around her as he stared at her for a second, making her feel that she was hanging in time, all breath and heartbeats suspended in one searing moment. Then his lips captured hers, not in any kiss that he had offered her before but with a driving demand that left her instantly trembling.

It was a kiss that seemed to have no end. A kiss that deepened until her arms tightened around his neck further, to hold herself upright, only relaxing when he moved her to his shoulder, her hair brilliant against his arm, her body tightly pressed against his.

'And just what were you trying to prove?' he asked thickly against her hair as he cradled her against him when her little cries had at last set her free from his devouring mouth. 'You were trying to prove that you were not a child? I already know that. No proof is necessary. Or were you trying to remind me that I am a man? Well—I know that too.'

He lifted his head and held her slightly away, still supporting her, his eyes cruelly intent.

'It is dangerous to practise on me,' he murmured softly. 'But it would be even more dangerous to practise on Alain. Dangerous for you and—for him!'

CHAPTER SIX

'I—I WASN'T practising, or—or anything,' Beth whispered, her face pale and frightened, the glow dying from her eyes at his anger. 'I'm sorry. I didn't mean to force you to—to...'

'You did not force me to anything!' he ground out irritably. 'I brought the whole thing on myself by teasing you. I have placed you in an invidious position and that was the result of it. You are very young, Beth, and I have been very possessive in my attempts to protect you. It is you who deserve my apologies.'

'No!' Beth was suddenly filled with a deep remorse. She had no right to intrude like this into his life. Before her arrival no doubt he was happy to live as he had always lived, and now he had a great responsibility. It drove her to a greater honesty than she had yet allowed herself even to look at in private thoughts. 'It wasn't your fault. I don't want to be an even greater burden on you and you have nothing to reproach yourself with at all. It was me. I was jealous—and...'

'Jealous!' He turned back to her, his eyes burning into hers as the colour she had lost flooded into her face again. 'I do not understand, Beth. Of whom were you jealous? I have done something that has made you jealous about Alain?'

'Oh, no, no!' Now that she had started there was no way out of it although her confession was now a painful thing. 'It has nothing to do with Alain. I—I was jealous a-about you ... Gabrielle ...'

101

Instead of anger there was a smile back in his eyes, and his hand rose towards her and then fell away without touching her as if he was very wary.

'I see, or at least, I think that I do.' He took a deep breath which did not seem to Beth to be too steady and then his hand came to her arm very gently. 'Come, *petite*, sit down for a minute.' He led her to one of the big and comfortable armchairs and sat her there, standing before her for a minute and then walking away to stand by the fireplace facing her, his arm resting along the mantelpiece, his eyes thoughtful on her face. 'What shall I say to you, Beth, that I have not already said many times?' he asked quietly. 'Gabrielle is part of my working life, has been a part of it for many years. We have much in common. There are many things that we discuss. This evening was an outing for you but for us, for Gabrielle, Alain and myself it was work, too. She may look as if all her thoughts are on her own appearance but those eyes were taking everything in tonight. She has the business at her fingertips.'

'Her eyes seemed to be mostly taking in me,' Beth said quickly and then bit her lip as she realised just how immature that sounded.

'Perhaps she, too, is jealous,' he said softly, smiling wryly as Beth quickly looked up. 'She is accustomed to my attention. She, too, is possessive, and I imagine that she does not like to think that you are here with me. You are very beautiful, you have the glow of extreme youth and—I spoil you.'

'I—I never noticed,' Beth muttered in embarrassment. 'You make me...'

'Do what I think is best for you,' he finished firmly. 'It is not easy to bring you safely from one kind of life to another, Beth, and, on the way, I have made mistakes.' He walked over and crouched down beside her looking up into her downcast face. 'You are a temptation to any man,' he said softly, 'and I am always aware of it. Teaching you to live is a very dangerous occupation and tonight, your little action of—frustration and anger took me by surprise. For a moment I forgot just who you are and who I am.'

'What else could you have done?' she murmured, determined that he should not take any of the blame.

'I could have laughed at you,' he told her quietly. 'I could have stepped back and laughed and sent you to your nice warm bed.'

'Why—why didn't you then?' Beth asked breathlessly, her eyes suddenly raised to his face, searching the contours of it with a beautiful bewilderment.

'I did not feel amused,' he confessed wryly. 'You offered your mouth sweetly and I took the gift greedily. I am no better than the next man, *chérie*.'

'You are!' she protested softly. 'You're very good to me, and sometimes I'm very annoying, I know.'

'In future,' he said deeply, pulling her to her feet, the discussion clearly over as far as he was concerned, 'I will try even harder to be good to you. Also, I will not kiss you again. I can see that it means too much to your English mind.'

A wave of pure disappointment washed across her face, and he laughed softly as he turned her to the door.

'Oh, you are delightful, *ma petite*,' he said amusedly. 'Perhaps I can offer myself an excuse.' He gave her a gentle little push to help her on her way. 'To your bed, Beth. It is time once again to curl up into a little ball and sleep. You have really used up a great deal of emotion tonight.'

'Gaetan?' She turned at the door and looked back at him with wistful eyes. 'Must I go out with Alain again? I enjoy the outings, but...'

'I think it is best if you do,' he said shortly, the
gentle amusement dying in his eyes. 'In September
you will begin at the university if you should so decide,
and then you will have your days filled very nicely.
There will be people there of your own age too, people
with your own interests. Going out with Alain is a
very good way of preparing you for other people with
no risk whatever. By September, your feet will be
firmly on the ground and you will have come to terms
with the idea that there is more in life than a rather
bad-tempered guardian!' He turned away rather
abruptly and there was nothing more to say.

All Beth felt was a kind of deep loneliness, and she
had brought things to a head by her idiotic actions.
All she had learned was that she was jealous of
Gabrielle and anyone else who had any claim on
Gaetan, and it only confirmed what he said. She had
been unloved and lonely, and she had fastened her
affections on Gaetan as soon as he had offered her
any kind of excuse. If that wasn't the action of a child,
what was?

As usual, he was correct and she had furthermore
caused him distress and embarrassment. All the same,
as she curled up in her bed, she remembered Gaetan's
lips on hers, demanding and hard, and the forbidden
feelings raged through her, making her moan aloud
and bury her head beneath the sheets. For the first
time in her life, something inside her had awakened
from a long sleep and it ate at her with a bitter and
sweet pain that kept her awake for many hours.

She saw little of Gaetan now, and she had no idea
where he spent his time when he was not working,
but common sense told her that he was with
Gabrielle. He had told her that he took Gabrielle out
frequently, and she imagined that it would not be a

platonic friendship. She tried her best to follow the code he had laid out for her. She never refused an outing with Alain, and she studied hard every day.

Alain, too, never seemed to tire of her company, and he was a cheerful and gallant companion, never making the slightest attempt to do more than occasionally hold her hand. She was glad of that. It had dawned on her very gradually that she did not wish to have anyone else kiss her, not after Gaetan, and she felt worried about that too. Maybe she was not quite normal. Maybe that was what being cut off from the real world did to people.

Whatever it was, she had no wish to experiment. It was a question that her mind asked and then refused flatly to look at any more deeply. She simply dared not think too much about it.

Her life went on with a well planned smoothness until one night, when without warning Alain's car stopped in a dark lane close to a village and refused to start, even after he had sworn at it ferociously under his breath.

'What's wrong with it?' Beth asked, her amusement at the incident fading into unease as the silence closed around them and the darkness made itself felt even in the car.

'God knows!' Alain exclaimed irritably. 'One thing I do know though, Gaetan is never going to believe this!'

'But it's not your fault!' Beth assured him in astonishment. 'I don't really see what you can do about it. Gaetan will be out anyway, he always is.'

'It is almost midnight,' Alain said ruefully. 'We are not too far off, but by the time I get this sorted out, Gaetan will be on the warpath.'

'Heavens! You're a grown man!' Beth laughed, her face highly amused now in the darkness.

'And you, *ma chère*, are a grown woman!' Alain shot back. 'Gaetan seems to think that you are nothing of the kind, however, and if I tell him the old story of the broken-down car and the lonely road he will take me apart. I step wide of Gaetan, he's dangerous, especially where you're concerned!'

'Well, it's only because he's responsible for me. He takes his duties very seriously,' Beth said in Gaetan's defence, trying to ignore the little trickle of fear that came at the thought of Gaetan's wrath.

'*Naturellement!*' Alain said with an ironic note in his voice that she could not understand. 'However, this is not helping. I will see what can be done.'

For a while he worked under the bonnet of the car with a flashlight while Beth sat in growing anxiety in the warmth of the car. Finally though she stepped out into the silent road and approached Alain.

'I've been thinking,' she began, her eyes on the rolled-up shirt-sleeves and the thick grease that seemed intent on covering his hands. 'We passed a little café back there, only a few yards back. There were people in it.'

'So?' Alain raised a slightly irritated face to her and she explained quickly.

'There's probably a phone. I could telephone Gaetan and tell him.'

'I suppose so,' Alain muttered, going back under the bonnet, 'Might as well be killed sooner than later. Get back in the car. I'll go along there.'

'I'll go!' Beth was off, running along the dark lane before Alain could react, and she ignored his calls. If Gaetan was going to be angry then she intended to get to him first and take some of the heat off Alain, and the café was very close by, she could see the lights even now.

It didn't look quite so light when she stepped inside and at the sight of her, dressed in a Vernais suit of blue silk, her hair a glorious disorder of gold around her face, her eyes alight and shining with the brisk run, all conversation stopped. Dismay flooded through Beth and she almost took to her heels then and there.

The place was filled with men, and although she told herself that they were merely country people having a final drink, she had to admit that they looked like ruffians of the worst type. She took her courage firmly in hand, though, and marched to the counter, her head high and a no-nonsense expression on her face.

'You have a telephone that I may use, *monsieur*?' she asked coldly as the patron, a fierce old man, stared at her grimly.

'*Oui, mademoiselle*, over at the back,' he said shortly. He neither asked questions nor offered help, and she was very glad of her fluent French as she went to the telephone and dialled Gaetan, praying that he was at home.

'Hello?' The deep voice washed over her like a benediction and she had to take a steadying breath to prevent herself from gabbling in a panic.

'Gaetan? It's Beth.'

She had no chance to say more because he was almost roaring into phone.

'What is the matter? What has happened? Answer me immediately!'

'Wait! I'm going to tell you if you'll give me the chance,' she pleaded. 'Alain's car has broken down and we're stuck on the road.' She gave him the name of the village and interrupted when he seemed about to set the phone on fire with wild oaths.

'Please, Gaetan!' she cried, raising her own voice. 'I'm all right but can you do anything to help? Alain can't get it started. I ran along to this café to use the telephone.'

'You ran along in the dark? *Ma foi!*' Everything she said seemed to make matters worse. 'Stay there until I come to get you! You hear me, Beth? Stay there.'

'Wait!' She really was in a panic now, afraid that knowing their location he would simply put the phone down and tear off leaving her here, the focus of all eyes, eyes that even now seemed to be burning holes in her back. 'I can't stay here, Gaetan.'

'You will! I will not have you out in the darkness alone!'

'I can't.' She was very much aware that everyone could hear her. She slipped into English desperately. 'Gaetan, it's an awful place. Let me run back to Alain,' she begged. 'This place is full of men and ...'

'How far away is the car?'

'A few yards only. Once round the bend in the road I'll see it,' she said desperately and he answered quickly.

'Very well, run back to Alain and sit in the car, lock the doors. I'll be there in minutes.' He put down the phone but not before she had heard him cursing softly, something about Alain and his bones, and she put the phone down and fled, not at all sure now what frightened her the more, Gaetan's rage or the unseemly looking men in the dirty café.

She raced back to Alain and received a telling off from him too for simply running off like that, but his voice took on less anger when she told him that Gaetan was on the way. They waited in an uneasy silence and Beth said softly, 'This is ridiculous. He's only one man.'

'That is the general impression that people have until they know him,' Alain offered scathingly. 'With time and study he reveals himself to be a whole group of men, all dangerous. I shall be forbidden to see you again.'

'Oh, rubbish!' Beth exclaimed, getting into the car as Alain once again delved into the mysteries of the engine. Her heart was beating like a hammer and Gaetan was not even here yet.

He came in a few minutes with a great blaze of lights and a great roar of noise, drawing up alongside and leaping out in a fury, and Beth too sprang out, wondering whether or not to throw herself in front of Alain who now stood with a murderous expression of his own, observing Gaetan in deep annoyance.

'Get in!' Gaetan opened the door of his low fast car and jerked his thumb at it, his eyes on Beth as if he was making an inventory of her appearance. She had no mind to disobey and slid into the seat with an anxious expression on her face that looked very much like guilt to any onlooker.

For a minute Gaetan stared at Alain and then his shoulders relaxed.

'I phoned for help on the way here,' he said tightly. 'The garage will be out to you at once. I'm taking Beth home.'

Alain managed a nod and reached for a rag to wipe his hands, a rag that was as dirty as the hands it was supposed to clean, and Gaetan waited no longer. He took off with a force that had her pressed back into the upholstery, her eyes on Gaetan's dark and angry face. She kept silent. Words were the last thing he would welcome right now and she knew it.

They were quite close to home as it turned out, near to one of the small villages that Beth had noted when she had first come to Paris with Gaetan, although in

the darkness the leafy roads did not now look quite
so inviting as they had done.

Gaetan was silent too, silent and angry, and even
when they stopped at the front of the house he said
nothing. There was no attempt to put the car away.
He simply abandoned it and led her inside, turning
her to the smaller of the two salons that the house
possessed and putting on the overhead lights as she
turned to face him.

He stared at her as he had never stared before, his
eyes as intent as they had been when he had arrived
to rescue her, although now, with the lights brightly
on her, she could tell that he was looking for any sign
that she had been manhandled.

'You are all right,' he said, and she couldn't tell
whether it was a statement or a question.

'I shall be when you stop frightening me to death,'
she said brightly in an attempt to lighten the
atmosphere.

'You are not concerned then that you have
frightened *me* to death?' he growled angrily, his gaze
riveted on her face. 'You were alone in a dark place
with Alain and then you were alone in a questionable
café with a whole gang of men who frightened you!
Mon Dieu! You realise do you not, that anything
might have happened to you before I could get to
you?'

'Nothing happened to me, Gaetan,' she pleaded in
a placating voice. 'It was all really a stupidity on my
part. I should have waited quietly with Alain until he
got the car fixed and then none of this would have
happened.'

'Worse would have happened!' he snarled. 'You
would have been out all night! Alain has no more
idea how to fix a car than he has of constructing a
hot-air balloon!'

'Then why did he fiddle about with it?' Beth asked with astonished eyes, her innocence making Gaetan turn angrily away.

'Perhaps he decided that it would be a good idea to find something for his hands to do!' he snapped scathingly. 'Or perhaps he was filled with cold panic when he realised that you were still out at midnight and likely to be out for a great deal longer.' He looked at her moodily and then said, 'Do you need a brandy?'

'No, thank you,' she said in a little dignified voice. 'Unless of course you intend to go on shouting at me.'

'I'm not shouting at you!' he roared and then looked decidedly abashed, a small flare of colour touching his high cheekbones. 'He—he didn't—touch you, did he, Beth?' he added softly, his eyes anxiously on her face.

'No!' Beth looked away and down at her toes, her own colour flaring, but her sense of humour got the better of her and she raised laughing eyes to his. 'I did think, though, that he was going to slap me when I got back from the phone.'

'He should not have let you go alone!' he said in an annoyed voice, staring at her until her knees began to shake.

'He didn't have much choice,' she assured him. 'I ran off.'

'Why, for heaven's sake? It was dark and lonely.'

'I know, that's why I ran off. I wanted to call you and—well...'

'You did not feel safe with Alain?' he asked suspiciously, and once again she had talked herself into trouble.

'Yes, but—but I wanted to—to...'

'To have me haring out to get you! You wanted to prove to yourself that I am at your beck and call, terrified that something will happen to you! You wanted to wield your female power!' he grated, stepping near in a threatening way.

'No!' She backed off and he stopped, his face relaxing and his lips twisting into a self-mocking smile.

'Well, nevertheless, it seems that I am at your beck and call and you do not seem to have very much difficulty in wielding your female power, even though it seems you do not understand it.' He tilted her face with one imperious finger and she looked at him defiantly, her face rosy and just a little stormy.

'Perhaps you had better go to your bed, Beth,' he said softly. 'We are both in an excited state and just on the edge of temper. To go off in two separate directions seems to be advisable right now. I will telephone the garage and see that Alain has been rescued. If he has not I will go back for him, now that there is no possibility of my killing him.' His dark eyes rested on her tremulous lips and he smiled slowly. 'For a while I think you will have a different escort—me.'

'Why?' she whispered, frightened when she realised that she wanted to be kissed very much indeed.

'To punish Alain, why else?' he asked drily. 'Goodnight, *chérie*.'

Beth almost ran from the room, her heart beating so fast that it was painful. He had called her darling again. He had been wild with rage that she was in danger and he had admitted that whenever she called he would race to her.

Stop being a fool, her mind told her. As to the endearment, Madeleine used it to Gaetan and to her. He probably hadn't even noticed, and of course he had raced to the rescue; he was, after all, her guardian. Still, he intended to take her out with him for a while and it was worth the small amount of fear she had suffered. Tomorrow she would ring Alain and make

it up to him. She would find a way to explain that
would not leave him hurt.

She curled up in bed and went to sleep with a smile
on her face, hugging the thought to her that for a few
days at least she would be with Gaetan. Admitting
that he was beginning to be the very centre of her
world, and that her desire to be free had slowly
vanished.

For a while the promised outings did not materialise,
but Beth knew that Gaetan was really busy with the
latest collection and she was quite content. For one
thing, he stayed at home as much as he could, though
what sort of trouble he thought she could get into
here under Madame Benoir's watchful eye she had
not the faintest idea. He took her on several trips to
the works and she saw Alain each time, though never
for more than a few minutes, as for one thing he too
was knee-deep in work, and for another she had no
wish to spoil the new and beautiful relationship that
she had with Gaetan.

Alain seemed to accept with no malice that she had
to stay close to Gaetan for the time being, and for
herself she was only too happy to do so, because their
relationship was now so close and comfortable that
she had never been happier in her life. Gone was the
old sardonic mood, the cruel, teasing tone, and
though, strictly speaking, he did not pay much attention to her, when he did it was with a warm and
gentle manner that made her feel well liked and safe.

She enjoyed too her growing friendship with Marie-
Annette because although the sharp-tongued and
businesslike woman was several years older than Beth,
she was easy to get on with and told her so much
about the work that Gaetan did. The fact that
Gabrielle was always somewhere in the background,

often to be seen with her head close to Gaetan and
her hand on his arm, was a thing that Beth had to
face whether she liked it or not.

Her eyes usually strayed in that direction, though,
and this did not escape the sharp-eyed gaze of Marie-
Annette.

'You are wondering about those two, eh?' she murmured one day, turning to see Gaetan's arm around
Gabrielle as he showed her something on one of the
benches. She pushed her great spectacles on to her
nose, getting on with the most complicated draping
on to a dummy the while. 'You are not alone there.
I very much doubt if Gaetan is involved with her, she
is not quite his type, it seems to me, but then again,
one never knows. He has been taking her out for some
considerable time. There are various opinions, you
can place your bets either side. One thing though is
sure, she has stayed the course longer than most and
I doubt if that is merely because she works here and
is good at her job.'

'Well, I suppose that a man like Gaetan has plenty
of lady-friends,' Beth offered, feeling like a traitor
but desperate to know where his feelings lay.

'Plenty is an understatement!' Marie-Annette
grunted through the pins in her mouth. 'They flock
around like sea gulls after a ship. He is, after all, very
handsome and virile, *n'est-ce pas*? Though I would
say that marriage is out of the question. Once was
enough for him, so they say.'

'He's married?' Beth actually felt the blood drain
from her face. He had said that he was not.

'You are not listening, *ma chère*!' Marie-Annette
said with a mocking frown, standing and removing
the pins from her mouth. 'When I gossip I expect
total attention. I said that once was enough for him,

note the word was. He is not married any more. She died.'

'Oh!' Beth hung her head. So he still loved someone who was no longer here. It saddened her so much that she just wanted to walk away. 'He must be so unhappy.'

'I would say that the only feeling he has is one of great relief,' Marie-Annette informed her evenly, stepping back to survey her creation. 'He married her when he was very young and foolish, and they were not really in love, I hear. She ran off and left him— of course he was not then rich and famous or she might have stayed and made him even more miserable. She died in a fire at a hotel where she was staying with her latest victim. I doubt if he even remembers her name, so do not go breaking your heart for him,' she added with a quick grin. 'He is more than capable of taking care of himself, and his heart is always under steady control. I often wonder whether he even has a heart!'

Gabrielle seemed to appear from nowhere and stood for a minute looking crossly at them both.

'Should you be making the latest models when there is an outsider in the place?' she asked Marie-Annette with a waspish look at Beth.

'I should be getting on with my work and that is exactly what I am doing!' Marie-Annette said. 'I suggest that you do likewise!'

'If you are worried about me, Mademoiselle Dubois,' Beth put in sharply, 'then I can save you any worries. I never go anywhere without Gaetan. We are together constantly now.'

It was spiteful she knew but somehow she couldn't help it and it hit home deeply. Gabrielle flushed with anger and stalked off on her very high heels, a trail of perfume marking her passage, and Marie-Annette laughed loudly, her eyes bright with speculation as she regarded Beth closely.

'Well, well!' she said softly. 'A blow below the belt I think, *ma chère*!'

Beth was glad that Gaetan appeared then to take her out to lunch. She did not have the courage at the moment to face either the speculation in Marie-Annette's eyes nor the questions that her own mind was beginning to ask very loudly.

'Been sharpening your tongue up again?' Gaetan asked softly as they drove off. 'I don't often see Gabrielle walk off from any argument with a red face.'

'There was no argument,' Beth assured him, keeping her eyes averted. 'She just seemed to be questioning whether or not I should be in the warehouse seeing so many secrets.'

'And of course you told her that you were to be trusted entirely?' he asked mildly.

'More or less,' Beth agreed, taking a great interest in the road at her side of the car.

'More, I would say from her looks. I suppose she deserved it and I suppose too that I shall hear all about it when I next see her. For you I am not at all worried. I know that you are well able to defend yourself.'

'That's not what you thought when you came to get me when Alain and I had broken down!' Beth said quickly, turning on him with flashing grey eyes. 'You said that I had to stay with you in future!'

'I said, for a while,' Gaetan corrected. 'The kind of trouble that I envisaged then cannot be escaped by the use of a sharp tongue, however well honed. You feel the necessity to see Alain again in the evenings?'

'No. I'm quite happy with things as they are!' said Beth quickly, feeling on decidedly slippery ground and not wanting to be foisted off on to Alain again.

'*Alors!* Tomorrow we will have a picnic. Just you and I.'

'A picnic?' Beth gazed at him in amazement. A picnic did not somehow fit into the general impression that she had of what Gaetan would find amusing, and her face showed her doubts.

'*Mais oui!* The French, *ma chère*, invented the picnic!' he stressed with a look of outrage that she knew was covering laughter. 'Do not imagine that we behave as you do when we dine out of doors. No soggy sandwiches and hot flasks of tea. We do things with style and...'

'Pizazz!' Beth finished, bursting into delighted laughter.

'*Vraiment!*' he said with a little dignified seated bow. 'You begin to understand us. I approve.'

Madame Benoir entered the spirit of things with a will, no doubt having been told by Gaetan that as a nation they were now under close observation and would have to be on their mettle. Gaetan and Beth left early with a bulging picnic basket that seemed to contain everything that would have done justice to a buffet lunch in a very splendid hotel, the wine and champagne included, and Beth sat with the wind blowing through her hair as they drove well out into the country, the windows of the car down in the warm air, the sun through the trees dappling the winding road as they climbed into the hills far away from the city.

She could have driven on for ever. Gaetan played tapes on the car's stereo system, and they rarely spoke unless he saw something to point out to her that would interest her, and she knew that he too was enjoying the day, the fresh air, the sunshine and the chance to relax away from Paris.

The car finally climbed for a long time through wooded hills where the flowers of summer were dotted beneath the trees, and when they finally pulled off the road, Beth found that they were parked on a high mound of a hill that overlooked a beautiful valley.

'It's lovely!' Beth exclaimed, getting out of the car and stretching like a cat, her slender arms above her head. 'Look! There's a river far away down there!'

'It is the Seine,' Gaetan told her. 'I used to come here long ago.'

'Oh! Well, I hardly thought that you had found this place by chance,' Beth said with a little smile, her mind going back to the days when he was married, the thought of him here with his wife taking some of the happiness from her face.

'I have never before brought anyone here,' he said softly, reaching into the boot for the basket. 'I like to think that this is my place alone.'

'Oh! I'm very honoured, then. Thank you!' Beth felt a rush of happiness and the feeling brightened her eyes, making her face glow, a fact that apparently he did not miss.

'You are—good to be with,' he said softly, looking at her for a moment. 'It is true that sometimes we fight. But when you are not battling with me, you are very tranquil and restful and I am content.'

'So am I,' Beth confessed, her face suddenly rosy with happiness and shyness.

'*Eh bien!* Then you may open the basket and serve lunch to your lord and master!' he announced, spreading a car rug and flinging himself on to it. 'I have done the driving. You can serve the lunch. It is all because of this "Women's Lib". Without it I might have been tempted to wait on you. Begin!'

It was a wonderful day. They ate and talked and sat for lengthy periods in silence listening to the breeze in the tall trees, the humming of insects and the far-away noises on the distant farms. To Beth it was heaven and she felt that she must do everything quietly, almost in stealth, in case this beautiful time should be in any way spoiled. She packed the remains of the lunch into the basket later as Gaetan sat smoking, his back against the sturdy base of a tree, and she glanced up with a smile as she felt him watching her. There was a very strange look in his eyes, but it was a look that did not in any way alarm her, and she looked back at him questioningly, saying nothing.

'I was thinking,' he said in answer to her unspoken question. 'I was thinking that you look—happy.'

'I am,' she assured him with a smile, getting on with the task she had begun, her slender and graceful hands neatly fitting things into place.

'Why are you happy?' he probed quietly.

'I don't know!' She looked up in surprise. 'Does it matter?'

'It does if I am to make sure that the happiness continues,' he stated simply.

'Does that matter either?' Beth asked, her heart beginning to take on a new and frightening rhythm.

'Perhaps. I would not wish you to remember your time with me as being a time of sadness after all. I know too that the age of twenty is fast creeping up on you. There will be then only one year left of—imprisonment. It is even less when you say it in months somehow. Twelve months and you will be free, rich, and on your own at last with nothing and nobody to stop you doing anything you want. You will be able to study or be idle, stay out all night, marry and have children if the mood takes you. You are looking forward to it?'

She sat back on her heels and looked at him with the same wide-eyed look in her clear grey eyes that he had somehow wished to avoid when he had first seen her. Sometimes she answered instantly when he questioned her, appearing to give no thought to her answers. Sometimes, though, she considered deeply any reply and the answers when they came then were the words of a person who had matured long before her time, a person who had wisdom beyond her years, and these answers left him always shaken and oddly bereft, wishing he had kept silent.

'I shall miss Paris and the things that I've learned here. I shall miss the laughter, the sights and smells, the flowers, the river, many little things.'

She looked away across the fields and woods to the shining strand of the river that wound like a ribbon of silver towards the distant sea. 'I shall miss you too,' she finished softly.

'Paris will always be here,' he said in a tight voice. 'So will I.'

'But I will be—elsewhere,' she said with a soft finality.

'You could stay here, Beth. There is a home for you here, always!' he reminded her deeply, but she shook her head and did not look up again.

'I think not. You've been good to me and I will always be grateful, and of course, I'll keep in touch with you, but I can't stay forever. I have my own country and I have to get back to a way of life there. Maybe I'll not even start university here. It seems quite pointless when there's only twelve months as you pointed out. Maybe I'll try to get into Cambridge. My Uncle John went there.'

She was trying really hard to let him see that he need not fear that he would be responsible for her for ever, but he took it very badly.

'I've spoiled your afternoon with my stupid questions!' he said savagely, getting to his feet and throwing the cigar as far as he could to ease the sudden fury that he felt with himself.

'No!' She knelt where she had been, her clear eyes looking up at him. 'It was something that had to be said. I've thought about it often, actually, but I didn't realise that it would have ever been in your mind.'

'Why, for God's sake?' he snapped and then sighed loudly, his hand running through his hair. 'No! Don't answer that! We shall only get into another of those question-and-answer situations and then it will be even worse.'

'There's nothing to be worse about, everything is perfectly splendid!' said Beth with a laugh, her gaiety forcing a smile to his stern face.

'Stop it!' he growled. 'You sound like my old nanny. Get up! I shall now show you another secret place, although I haven't decided yet if you deserve such a treat.'

He pulled her to her feet, keeping her hand in his, and she was grateful to be spared any more interrogations. It had taken all her courage to be light-hearted and to say that she would leave Paris and Gaetan. The truth was that she never wanted to leave, and she had known that for days and days, weeks even. She blinked back the tears that were threatening and practised a smile in case he should turn to look at her.

CHAPTER SEVEN

THE secret place was approached through thickly growing bushes, and it looked as if nobody had been here for years; Gaetan said that they probably had not as it was so far off the beaten track. He had to fight his way forward in some places, but apparently he was determined, and her burst of unhappiness eased as she struggled behind him, wishing mightily that she had come in jeans to face this assault-course.

They finally broke through into a clear area and rising in front of them was an old stone tower, crumbling in places but still sturdy-looking and very high.

'What is it?' Beth asked, the old unease rising inside her as she looked up at the tall building that seemed to be trying to touch the sky.

'It was once part of a castle,' Gaetan informed her, his voice as pleased as a boy's to be showing her this. 'I've never been able to find out much about it but I used to spend hours here, and it is certainly the one remaining keep of a very large castle that overlooked this valley. Come inside.' He tugged on her hand, feeling her reluctance but not looking round at her. 'It's quite safe. If it had not been I would not have brought you here.' If he had looked round he would have seen her suddenly pale face, but he was too intent on sharing his treasure with her and he moved inside, taking her with him, assuming her reluctance to be something other than what it really was.

But it was dry and secure inside the tower, the only sign of the outdoors the occasional slits in the walls, and Beth's fears subsided as her interest grew.

'It is quite possible that this is one of the remaining keeps of a castle of the Knights Templar,' Gaetan told her, his face intrigued as they both looked up at the walls. 'They were welcomed in France for a time after they left the Holy Land, but as they always seemed to shroud themselves in mystery it would take a great deal of dedication to track them down.'

'Are you interested?' Beth asked, lowering her voice to accommodate the silence.

'Yes,' he whispered back, grinning at her in the semi-darkness. 'The floors are still intact,' he continued, using a normal voice now, 'and you can see where the fires used to be. Come and look!'

Somehow, Beth found herself climbing the stone steps cut into the walls. In places they had to bend double, and it might have been the concentration of this that kept her mind totally off the fact that they were steadily climbing upwards.

Then Beth's world dissolved into panic and nightmare. They stepped out on to the battlements, low and sturdy, it was true, but no barrier to her fright. The farms and distant river now looked like so many toys, each path leading down the hills clearly defined and seemingly miles below them, and the nightmare had only begun. As always she was drawn to the terror, her steps dragging but constant, her eyes glazed with fear as she saw herself falling and falling, turning over and over in the air to go on without end, downwards to her death.

'Beth!' She swayed dizzily and Gaetan's sharp call came in time to halt her as she neared the edge of the low wall, his hand on her arm gripping tightly. '*Mon Dieu!* What are you doing?' He spun her round to

face him and his words died for a second in his throat.
'You are faint?' he questioned fiercely, holding tightly
to her, but her speech centres were frozen as usual
and her eyes did not see him clearly, all her body was
stiff with shock, paralysed into rigidity.

'Vertigo! *Dieu!*' He pulled her to him and held
tightly to her for a few seconds and then carefully and
steadily, talking to her all the time, he edged her
towards the stairs, backing down in front of her,
shutting out the sight of any drop, his hands on her
hips hard and warm, pulling gently, forcing her locked
limbs to respond as they steadily retraced their steps
to the bottom room.

She began to shake then, quivering like someone
with a fever, her skin cold with shock, and he pulled
her into his arms, rocking her against him, murmuring soothing words that he knew she could not
really hear, until finally she leaned against him, weak
and trembling but back to her normal self, out of the
frightened rigidity that had gripped her.

He swung her up into strong arms and strode
outside then, forcing his way back towards the car,
not listening to her weak little pleas.

'Put me down, Gaetan. I can walk. It's too difficult
here.' He did not answer and she went on pleadingly.
'Please!'

'No! Let me hold you! Turn your face against my
shoulder in case any of the thorns cut you.' He would
not listen so she did as he said, her arms clinging to
his neck, her face hidden against him until they were
once again by the car, the keep well out of sight behind
the tall and thickly wooded slope.

With obvious reluctance he let her feet touch the
ground, but held her tightly still, his fury with himself
very evident.

'Today will be a day to remember,' he rasped harshly. 'I have spoiled your happiness with my stupid questions and then I have almost led you to your death!'

'No! It—it's been a beautiful day!' she choked, the tears flowing down her face now that the last stages of her shock were upon her. 'I've loved it!'

'You are an idiot!' he said thickly, sitting once again with his back to the trees and taking her with him. 'I have always suspected it. Come here!'

He pulled her into the circle of his arms and she came willingly, a little sigh escaping her as she rested against the hard power of his chest, feeling his head come close as he rested his face against her hair.

'Why did you not tell me, Beth?' he asked in an anguished voice. 'Why did you allow me to drag you up there when one little word would have saved all this?'

'It's hard to explain,' she sighed. 'You'll think I'm even more of an idiot when I tell you that I almost forgot. Outside, looking up, I know very well what will happen and nothing would then make me face the height. But it was dark in there, safe, almost cosy, and I never even thought of what would happen when we stepped out into the daylight. I didn't even realise that we would be stepping out. Suddenly, we were there and it was too late.'

'You could have yelled out to me, straight away before it caught you too badly. You could have let me know!' he protested quietly but she buried her face into his shirt and shook her head.

'I try not to tell anyone,' she confessed in a mere whisper, 'but I'm glad that you know now.'

'I should think so too!' he grunted crossly, tightening his arms around her. 'And now that I know, let's have it all. Tell me how long this has been going on and what has been done about it at this splendid school you attended.'

'It started soon after my parents were killed in the air-crash,' she said, trying to sit up and being firmly pulled back against him. 'I'm too imaginative, or so they say. To me it wasn't just an air-crash, it was people flying into the air, falling down with nothing to help them. To me my parents didn't die in the plane, they simply fell, and I've never been able to go anywhere high since then, even though now I know better.'

'Ah, then that is why you said so stubbornly that you would not fly to Paris when I came and captured you,' he said, tilting her face and smoothing her last tears away with his gentle fingers. He suddenly stilled as a thought came to him. 'It is also why you refused to go with me to Rome and Madrid.'

'Yes.' She looked away from his brilliant gaze. 'I— I wanted to but...'

'And I thought that you hated the sight of me,' he said softly, laughter back in his voice. 'You are too secretive, *ma petite*, too secretive by far. Never mind though, I will take you to Paul and he will recommend someone who will sort you out in no time at all.'

'No!' She sprang away from him and on to her feet before he could stop her. 'No! I'll see nobody! I've had enough of prying into my life, into my mind!'

He got to his feet and came to stand behind her, reaching for her shoulders, now tense and unyielding, pulling her back against him even though she was reluctant to come.

'I think that there is more that I should know, even at the risk of being accused of prying into your mind and your life,' he insisted quietly. 'Sit down again, Beth, and tell me who has pried and what they decided after their prying.'

She sank obediently to the ground and this time he did not touch her, instead he sat down away from her where he could see her face and she curled her legs round her and leaned on her hand, staring down into the valley that now held no fears.

'Naturally, when they found out that I had such severe vertigo the school called Uncle John and tried to do something about it,' she began and then she turned urgently to him, her eyes pleading. 'Do you know what it's like to be different, Gaetan? Do you know what it's like to be slightly at the side of the world and not quite in it? I was an orphan, I was rich in my own right even before Uncle John left me more. I was very clever without any real effort and I had a—a disease!'

'It is not a disease!' he snapped, fixing her with a firm stare. 'It is a phobia!'

'Phobia, disease, what does it matter,' she said bitterly. 'I had psychiatrists, long talk sessions, endless reports. If I had been going home afterwards, even to Uncle John, maybe it would have felt different. I simply went to my room, though, with nobody there to talk things over with me.' She sighed deeply. 'I only wanted to be normal!'

'You are normal,' Gaetan said quietly. 'There must be plenty of girls even now in schools dotted around England who are without parents and who have difficulties. Anyway, you are just very, very special.'

'I've no desire to be special!' she snapped, her face angry. 'And I will not see anyone about this vertigo. Let it rest, Gaetan. Just leave me as I am.' She stared into his eyes until he seemed to be drowning in her silvery gaze and his lips tightened as he stood and pulled her also to her feet.

'All right! You are entitled to do whatever you wish about your problems. Just see that you do not again seek danger. Then it becomes my problem. I have problems enough.' He turned to the car and opened the door. 'Let's go home.'

'Is—is that all you're going to say?' she asked, realising that she had angered him but not quite sure how.

'Why, yes! What more is there to say? You have made a decision and I can see the reason for it. I can also understand your fear both of heights and of prying people. Many people have problems, and often they are simply ironed out in the normal and natural surroundings as time goes on. You did not have normal surroundings because you had nobody to turn to, those who would have helped were shut out of your life by your own wishes. When you decide to return to this world, no doubt there will be somebody waiting to take up your burden and sort it out for you. Clearly that person is not me. Another decision you have made for yourself.'

'You always misunderstand me!' Beth said, turning away from the car and staring out across the fields. 'Sometimes you seem to do it deliberately.'

'That is not true,' he said sharply, turning her round and urging her towards the car, closing the door firmly behind her and gathering the remaining things into the boot. 'When it is your birthday next week I intend to give a dinner party,' he said, continuing as if this were the real point at issue and clearly deciding that anything else was not now to be discussed further. 'It will give you the chance to act as my hostess, as befits your position in my life, and also it will be a good way of celebrating your birthday.'

'What?' She turned to look at him with wide-open eyes. 'What are you doing? Humouring me as if I were a madwoman?'

'No, I suppose that you did realise that it is your birthday next week?'

'I suppose so,' she said indifferently. 'Birthdays are something that I've never bothered with.'

'That is because it is not up to the birthday person to bother about it. Other people normally tend to insist upon that kind of celebration, and I insist. From now on you will have a birthday just like anyone else and please do not bother to argue. After this there will be one more only and then you can return to your normal indifference.'

'I can't really see what I've done to anger you,' Beth said miserably, clenching her hands in her lap and looking down.

'You have not angered me,' he said tightly. 'You have just made it clear that I can protect and guide you only as far as you will allow. There is nothing I can do about it, apart from giving you a good shaking, and I hesitate to do that. You have enough worries without any major disturbance. If I simply go ahead and make appointments for you and insist that you keep them, then we will be once again in the situation where you are filled with resentment. I do not want that, therefore I shall ignore this new problem and simply beg you to take care.'

'Sometimes you are very hard.' Beth turned away from him and looked out of the car window, wondering what had happened to her happy day.

'Sometimes it is a necessity!' he said, his eyes firmly on the road. 'Nevertheless, you will have a dinner party for your birthday and it will serve the purpose of both celebrating the event and introducing you to the finer points of being a gracious hostess in my house.'

The end of the discussion had been reached and he said nothing further, leaving Beth to her own thoughts which were not at all happy. He was so many things to her that sorting out her feelings was impossible. He protected her, raged at her, became angry with her unexpectedly and left her feeling utterly alone, more alone than she had ever felt before. He excited her too, her cheeks flushed as she thought about that. There were times when she simply just wanted to be wrapped in his arms and feel his kisses. She knew without any experience whatever that the satisfaction she craved would only come from Gaetan. It was not and never would be possible. She was not even sure what the empty feeling inside her meant. She sighed and stared straight ahead, her little sound drawing his attention.

'You bring out both the best and the worst in me, Beth,' he said into the silence, 'but you know that I do not wish to see you unhappy, do you not?'

'Yes, I know that,' she answered softly. 'I also know that I'm difficult and I'm grateful that...'

'Gratitude is not a thing that I really need,' he murmured. 'Come here, *petite*. We will make it up, eh?' He reached out an arm and drew her to his side and she came willingly and softly, snuggling into his shoulder with a little sigh that brought a smile at last to the tight lips. '*Alors!* The day ends well after all. We will forget our differences and remember the good things, and when we get back, I will play cards with you until dinner time.'

'All right,' she said, secretly biting her lip. She had grown quite accustomed to his brotherly attitude when he spoke to her. He seemed to forget the times that he had held her in an entirely different way but she could never forget. Rather than play cards, she would have gone on driving with him like this until they reached the end of the world.

*   *   *

Madame Benoir was delighted to hear that there was to be a dinner party and began arranging it as soon as Gaetan told her, sitting in the kitchen with pencil and paper, her face thoughtful as Beth walked in during the week.

'I am as excited as a girl!' she confessed. 'There were many parties here not too long ago. It will be good to get back into the old ways.'

'I suppose that I have interrupted the old ways,' said Beth ruefully, but Madame Benoir simply got up and poured Beth a coffee, setting it down on the table and sitting down with her own coffee for the little break that they had recently taken to having together in the middle of the morning.

'Yes, I suppose to be truthful that is the case,' she admitted quietly, 'but do not be too hard on yourself. Monsieur Vernais is much happier these days than he used to be, he has less of a nightlife too, and that, in my opinion, is all to the good. There was a time when I expected to see him kill himself with so much searching after illusion.'

'Illusion?' Beth looked up at her, her cup cradled in her hands, her eyes puzzled, and Madame Benoir pursed her lips.

'Oh, you know, Mademoiselle Beth, chasing the very thought of happiness. He is much more settled now, you have given him a focus for his life. It is, I expect, like suddenly having acquired a younger sister. He has other things to think about now, not just work and enjoyment. Happiness cannot be chased, it grows from the inside.'

'You are a philosopher, *madame*!' Beth laughed, bringing a smile to the face before her, but adding softly, 'Perhaps he missed his wife.'

'That one!' Madame Benoir snorted scornfully. 'He married her because he needed a wife, or so he seemed to have convinced himself. From the first, they quarrelled like enemies. He was not then rich and established, you understand, and she wanted everything, everything except Monsieur Vernais. It was a great mistake and we were all very pleased when she left. There was not one tiny bit of tenderness in her, only greed and a great desire to attract men. He was well rid of her, she would have ruined his life!'

'Well, he has taken on a great responsibility with me,' Beth commented sadly. 'I frequently annoy him.'

'It is only natural!' Madame Benoir said in surprise. 'To be feminine is to be annoying very often. At least it is clear that you care for him. I hope that he will be content for a while. I have often thought that he was contemplating another disastrous marriage. Mademoiselle Dubois is not at all suitable for him but she has a very nasty habit of clinging. He could be fooled. There!' She stood swiftly straightening her apron. 'I am gossiping about my employer and that is very wrong. Still, I have known him for a very long time and we all love him, *n'est-ce pas*?'

'Yes,' Beth murmured, wishing she had never been in the kitchen at all, her face suddenly pale as she went to her room to sit and stare at the wall, making no move to do anything.

Love him? Was that what it was that was wrong with her? Was that why she could think of very little else nowadays but his face, his voice, the warmth of his arms? Was that why painful and forbidden feelings flooded through her every time he held her? She got up and went to stare out of the window, seeing nothing but the misery that raced around in her mind like a wild animal seeking refuge.

To love Gaetan in any other than a friendly way would be to invite disaster. He was experienced, pol-

ished, way out of her reach, and he thought of her
as little more than a teenager who was quickly growing
up to be a woman. He had enough problems coping
with her as it was. She could never let him see that
there was another problem growing inside her that
would have to be faced one day.

She turned back to her books, trying to lose herself
in her studies, and when Gaetan returned and called
in to see why she was not using the library as usual
she merely mumbled at him, not even looking up,
giving the impression that once again she was antagonistic, and he walked off, slamming the door, making
it quite clear that he intended to let her get on with
it. Maybe it was time to allow Alain back on to the
scene? He stood in the library, irresolute, and then
poured himself a drink, tossing it off without even
tasting it. What the hell was he going to do about
her?

By the time that Beth's birthday came around, it was
clear to him that it had not been just a momentary
mood. He hardly saw her except at dinner, and after
a few evenings when they hardly spoke and Beth was
withdrawn and far away, he took to dining out again
with Gabrielle, anything to escape from the look of
distant and aloof indifference on her face.

As to the party, Beth had been living in dread of
the event, and when she got ready for the dinner on
the night of her birthday, her hands were actually
shaking, and making up was an unusually difficult
task. She did not know what Gaetan really expected
of her. He had been distant for days and she hardly
ever saw him. He was out with Gabrielle most nights,
and often when she came into the library to collect a
book he was talking to Gabrielle on the phone, his

voice warm and intimate, his manner telling her that
she intruded.

She sighed and dressed with care; at least that was
easy. She had been saving her best-loved gown for an
occasion and this seemed to be it. The creamy silk
clung to her waist and hips, billowing out into the
full-flowing skirt, the low halter neck leaving her
shoulders and back free of covering.

She left her hair loose, brushed into a shining cloud
around her shoulders, and looked at herself critically.
She looked good, a little pale, and she knew that she
had lost weight since she had discovered her true
feelings for Gaetan, but nevertheless she looked good.
She went downstairs, realising that she did not even
know who had been invited, biting her lip when she
thought how remiss of her this was, to have shown
so little interest in an event that had been planned for
her. She and Gaetan were now like strangers.

The sound of voices drew her to the big salon where
he seemed to have begun to entertain the guests in her
absence, another crime to be set against her. She
should have been down earlier instead of hiding away
like a frightened child. She took a deep breath, raised
her shining head and walked into the brightly lit room.

It seemed to be full of people and at her entrance
all talk stopped as they turned towards her. Then
Madeleine detached herself from a group at the far
end of the room and sailed towards her, her arms
outstretched.

'Happy birthday, *chérie*!' she called, breaking the
silence, and then the others called to her too, wishing
her a happy birthday, kissing her cheeks and making
the awkward moment pass.

Her eyes searched for Gaetan, finding him at once
as he stood tall and handsome by the fireplace that

was now filled with the flowers of summer. He raised
his glass in salute, his dark eyes intently on her, noting
the pallor of her face, the bruised look about her eyes,
her very brittle slenderness. She seemed to be so withdrawn these days, and he had to fight hard to keep a
frown from his face.

'Now that the hostess has arrived, we can eat,' he
said sardonically, bringing a quick flare of colour to
her cheeks, and Madeleine slid an arm into Beth's.

'Ignore him, *ma chère*,' she whispered. 'He is
abominable at times and he has with him an abominable companion. Had I known that Gabrielle Dubois
was to be here I would have sent my apologies and
bought you a bigger present to make up for it.'

Beth had noticed that Gabrielle was here, in fact
she had been so stunned by it that she had failed to
notice that there were also Marie-Annette and Alain.
Clearly, Gaetan had been in a fix as to who to invite,
as so few of his friends knew her.

Alain joined them and slid his arm around Beth in
a possessive manner, making the most of the fact that
it was permissible on her birthday.

'I am here, you know!' he announced in a loud and
amused voice.

'Oh, Alain! I was so confused when I realised that
I was late that I really haven't had time to look
around.'

'It should not be necessary!' he stated with a wry
and amused face. 'What do they say? Across a
crowded room? You should have seen me instantly.'

It was Gaetan she had seen, and his eyes again met
hers as he heard Alain's remark. Oh, God! Was she
that obvious? He must never know what was eating
at her, making every day a misery. She laughed gaily
at Alain and by skilful management she kept him at

her side as they went into the long and beautiful
dining-room, where she greeted her guests like a
mature and well practised hostess, her hand on Alain's
arm.

For Beth, the meal was a small nightmare, and she
hardly knew what she said during the course of it.
She sat at one end of the table, Gaetan at the other,
and there was no way that she could escape his glittering gaze. There was no way either that she could
fail to see Gabrielle, so obviously with Gaetan, taking
all his time, perfectly at home here. She knew this
house and this man only too well.

After the meal, when Gaetan strolled over to the
group she was talking to in the salon, Gabrielle
clinging to his arm, Beth could face no more. She slid
away with a murmured excuse, drifting from the room
unnoticed, her silky dress whispering around her
ankles. She found the french windows in the smaller
salon that was not in use and slipped out into the
cooler night air. Her skin was hot and dry, her hands
trembling. She could not bear to see Gaetan with
Gabrielle for one more minute.

Her tears were so very close to the surface as she
tried to come to terms with her feelings, trying to look
at things rationally. It was no good whatever. There
was nothing rational about her feelings for Gaetan.
It had grown on her without her knowledge. The
safety of his possessiveness, the realisation that he
cared what happened to her, the comfort of his arms.
These things were new, so unexpected that she had
simply sunned herself in them, taking his harsher moments in her stride in order to have these new and
wonderful comforts. The rest had been there almost
all the time. She knew that now. Her stunned and
bewildered feelings when she had first seen him had

been a warning signal that she had been too inexperienced to recognise. Now, it was all too late. She had no idea what to do. There was nobody to tell.

Footsteps behind her made her jump guiltily, but she had not expected to escape from Alain for long. She didn't even turn.

'Sorry that I walked out, Alain,' she said brightly. 'I was feeling a little too hot.'

'It will disappoint you, I know, but it is not Alain, regrettably, it is only I.' Gaetan's cool and cynical voice sent shivers of apprehension through her and she turned with a half-smile on her face.

'Oh, I expected Alain to come chasing out. I didn't expect to see you, Gaetan.'

'I assumed that he would be here too,' Gaetan said with a look of disapproval. 'However, I did not come to spy on you. What you do at twenty years of age is none of my business so long as it is reasonably proper. I came to tell you that very soon everybody will be wanting to give you a present. It is our normal custom to wait until after dinner. I would not like to have to come and drag you from Alain's arms to present you slightly dishevelled to your guests.'

'You know that there's nothing like that between Alain and me,' Beth said quietly. 'Why are you trying to hurt me?' she added in a whisper, walking further away into the garden. The moonlight turned her dress to silver and her skin to a pale, translucent softness.

'I am not trying to hurt you!' he said tightly, following her and coming to stand facing her, his eyes on her delicate face.

'Please don't ever try then,' she said with an attempt at light-heartedness. 'The experience would probably kill me!'

She suddenly shivered and he reached out to touch her arm, running his hand along her skin.

'You are cold! What are you doing out here anyway?'

'I thought I was out here to meet Alain,' she said, her eyes challenging him as she looked up.

'Stop arguing!' he said in a tightly controlled voice. 'Come here and get warm!' He reached for her and opened his jacket, drawing her into the warm circle of his body, feeling her trembling against him. 'Now take all the air you need and then let us get back!' he ordered. 'This is not a very good idea!'

'It was your idea,' she murmured, her shaking not at all lessening as she tried to step away but was drawn inexorably back to the temptation of his warmth.

'One of us has to be sensible,' he said in a low voice. 'Obviously, it will never be you.' He held her closely until she relaxed, her head falling to his chest as his hands began to wander over her chilled arms and her tense back. 'What am I going to do with you?' he muttered against her hair. 'You are so very difficult to manage. Sometimes it is almost impossible. Do you know that?'

He pulled her tightly to him and she could not resist the urge to wind her arms around his waist and snuggle against him, her face against his heavily beating heart. 'So, you are my friend again?' he said in a low and driven voice. 'After days of silence you are back here.'

'I try not to upset you, truly,' whispered Beth shakily.

'Truly!' he repeated thickly. 'You have no idea what goes on in life unless it is right under that small and beautiful nose.'

Beth lifted her head, drawn by the sound of his vibrant voice, and he looked down at her before dropping a kiss on the tip of her nose, his breathing quickening when she simply went on looking at him, keeping her face tilted to his.

'*Mon Dieu!*' he whispered huskily. 'You know what you invite?'

He did not wait for a reply; instead his lips brushed her cheeks, and when she turned her head just a little, he was waiting for her, his mouth capturing hers with a yearning hunger that sent waves of shock through her, igniting flames in both of them.

She kissed him back with a kind of desperation, tightening her arms around his waist as he clasped her in an almost cruel grip that allowed for no escape even if she had wanted one. She didn't want to escape, though; fire ran through her with a consuming and fierce flame as his hands, possessive and demanding, moulded her against him, locking them together, turning her into a being she didn't even recognise.

The magic was all-consuming and she seemed to be on another level of existence beneath the burning onslaught of his lips, her tiny cries of excitement and desperation at last forcing him to lift his head.

He held her against him for a moment, giving her time to recover, but the soft and anguished cries did not stop and he tilted her face to the moonlight, his eyes burning down at her.

'Don't do that!' he commanded harshly, his hands restless on her slender body. 'You are signalling a need that I cannot ever fulfill, *tu comprends*?'

She lifted her head and shook it wildly, her hair flying out and brushing his face, and he caught her to him with a low groan, cradling her head and kissing her trembling lips with a tenderness that his voice had never suggested was there.

'Come inside, slip up to your room and recover a little and then we will see what you have in the way of presents,' he coaxed, his own voice by no means steady.

'Somebody will see me,' she whispered, stepping away from him and brushing her hand across her face in a little gesture that touched his heart.

'Nobody has the least idea where you are,' he assured her, his arm coming around her as he guided her back to the house.

'You knew,' she said softly, still shaking in the aftermath of her first real taste of desire, a deep shame beginning to wash over her at the wanton behavior that had driven Gaetan to kiss her like that.

'When you came through the small salon you left the door open, and as this is the only room with windows that lead out here, I knew very well where you were.'

'And you thought that I was with Alain,' she said miserably.

'I did not,' he answered in an even voice, clearly returned to normal long before her, although it had not meant so much to him.

'Anyway,' she sighed, 'if you could see the door open then so could anyone else.'

'It is no longer open,' he said quietly. 'As I came through, I locked it.'

'Why?' she asked with a breathless waiting in her voice that had him urging her on faster.

'Do not even think of that!' he said roughly, leading her into the empty hall. 'It is something that I am trying to forget.'

CHAPTER EIGHT

ONCE in her room, Beth sank to the bed, trying to recover and return to some sort of normality, a deep and painful aching inside her that refused to be quelled. But there was no time to sit and brood over the magical and frightening time in the garden, no time to be filled with remorse over her behaviour. She knew that her own longing and actions had driven Gaetan to something that he would regret, something that he regretted now, and things would never be the same again.

Soon, very soon she would have to leave, and there was no way that it could be left until her next birthday. She would have to persuade him to let her go back to England. He would probably be only too glad to let her go now. She was a danger to both of them.

Her own appearance shocked her. Her eyes were over-bright, her mouth too full and pulsating, and there was a new feeling inside that made her slender body seem voluptuous to her own eyes. She would step into the brightly lit room and they would all know! A wave of panic washed over her when she thought of what it would mean to Gaetan and she lingered unforgivably.

He came to fetch her, knocking softly on the door and coming in when she could not even bring herself to answer.

'Hurry! I cannot keep them waiting any longer!' His face was harsh and tight, no lingering sign of passion in his eyes, and she looked at him helplessly.

141

'I—I can't! Tell them that I've got a headache! Please, Gaetan!'

'No!' He strode forward and grasped her, lifting her to her feet. 'You must face them and live through it, my girl. You are a woman now and you should be quite capable of facing the eyes of anyone!'

'Facing the consequences of my actions, you mean?' she murmured unhappily her face flushed as she looked away.

'No, facing the consequences of *my* actions!' he snapped impatiently. 'I have told them that you felt a little faint and they believed it; it is in fact true,' he said ironically. 'Come,' he added in a kinder tone, 'there is not much longer left to be brave. Let us go down and get it over with.'

There was no alternative and she faced them, grateful to Gaetan that for the rest of the evening he stayed at her side, wondering how she was going to tell him that she wanted to go back to England.

'Some time this week, there will have to be a trip to the coast,' Alain reminded Gaetan as they all had coffee before leaving. 'I cannot say that I am looking forward to it, but then again, it has to be done. Do you wish me to go alone?'

'No!' Gaetan was clearly not anxious to discuss work at this late hour and his voice was touched with irritability. 'Naturally I will need to go too and it will be a good idea if Gabrielle were to come along. I shall need her.'

'For what will you need me, *chéri*?' Gabrielle was there at once, sitting beside Gaetan on the settee, making the most of the fact that he had spoken her name. She had not been too pleased that he had spent all his time with Beth since she had come back into the room, and it had shown on her face.

'It is the new material,' Gaetan said, glancing at her with a smile. 'Alain will need to make the trip and so will I. I would like you to go too.'

'Shall we be staying the night?' Gabrielle said, managing to attract the attention of most of the guests and making it sound like a private assignation between her and Gaetan.

'We shall stay the night,' Gaetan said smoothly, adding, 'As it is at the coast, we may as well make it into a small holiday. We will travel early one day and return the next evening.'

'Then I shall take my own car and desert you!' Alain cut in with an irritability of his own. 'A trip to the sea I can well do without. I will leave you two to paddle alone!'

'Oh, we shall not be alone,' Gaetan said into the embarrassed silence that followed these disclosures. 'I have every intention of taking Beth with me. The weather is good and she will enjoy the sea air.'

'Ah, well,' Alain said, smiling at Beth. 'In that case...'

'I haven't said that I'll go!' Beth burst out, her eyes on Gaetan's aloof face.

'But you will, *petite*,' her guardian assured her tauntingly. 'I shall persuade you. In any case, Alain will be there and you can paddle together.'

They stared at each other for a second, everyone else in the room forgotten, and then Gabrielle said in an over-bright voice.

'I think that she deserves it! After all, *chéri*, you are the only one who has not given her a present. Is this her present then, a few hours by the sea with Alain?'

Beth's face flushed painfully at the taunt and Gaetan reached out for her wrist in a lazy manner, pulling her to the settee beside him, the lack of room

now that Gabrielle was sprawled along there making
Beth sink down very close to him.

'No,' he said quietly. 'I was merely saving my gift
to give to her later, but I do not want her thinking
that I have forgotten. I will give it to her now.'

He reached into his breast pocket and took out a
long, thin leather case and as everyone came intrigued to look, he withdrew a small and delicate gold
watch, taking her wrist again and fastening it for her.
It was exquisite, and she could only stare at it as
everyone gasped in admiration.

'Do I not deserve a kiss of thanks?' Gaetan murmured, loud enough for everyone to hear, and her
grey eyes met his, a soft reproach in them as she
reached to kiss his cheek. His hands tightened on her
wrist, his fingers softly caressing on the wildly beating
pulse there, and she couldn't read what was in his
eyes but for a second there seemed to be an almost
blinding flash of tenderness.

It was not far to the coast after all and, as they took
the Rolls-Royce, the journey seemed to be over
quickly. This time, there was no suggestion that she
should be at Gaetan's side, because he himself placed
her firmly in the back with Alain, an arrangement
that suited everyone, including Beth. She had come
to terms with her situation. She loved Gaetan, wanted
him, but it was never going to be possible. He had
told her that in the garden, and his stiff, unbending
attitude today had assured her that he meant it.

After this week, next at the latest, she would leave
Paris and go home. The very word home made her
more than ever unhappy. She felt that there would
now never be a home for her except with Gaetan and
that was not possible. The very way he was talking
to Gabrielle, their conversation ranging from the

business to the fashion world, to moments of light-hearted bantering, making her realise more than ever that she was not of his world and would never fit in.

The resort was small and uncrowded, with just one rather splendid hotel, and Alain told her that this place had very little to offer except very good shops. The tourists made for the brighter lights further down the coast. The mill was here, though, that supplied some of their materials and they had come to place orders for the following spring, working far ahead of time as usual.

'Are you coming to the mill with us?' Gaetan asked after lunch when Beth had gone up to her room.

'No, thank you,' she answered quietly. 'I'll only be in the way. I'll walk along the sand for a while.'

'No!' He stepped into the room and fairly bristled with hostility. 'It is not a crowded resort, in fact, to call it a resort at all is stretching the imagination. There are very deserted places here along the coastline and I do not wish you to wander alone!'

'I'm a big girl now!' Beth turned away unhappily from his annoyed face but he did not give an inch.

'You are young and beautiful and therefore always at risk!' he ground out harshly. 'I did not imagine that you would want to come to the mill, not because you would be in the way but because you would probably be bored. There are, however, some very chic shops here, and you can buy yourself a couple of bikinis, a beach wrap and anything else that takes your fancy. I have yet to meet a woman who does not like to gaze in shop windows and spend money.'

He peeled off a roll of notes and thrust them at her but she backed off as though they were hot.

'I don't want to spend your money, Gaetan, thank you!' she said angrily.

'*Mon Dieu*, you are asking for trouble!' he snarled, towering over her. 'Take the money and spend it! If it worries you then I will send you a bill when you are in possession of your inheritance. I will see that it contains a detailed account of your meals in my house, your clothes and everything else that you are concerned about! Write down your debts to me and we will settle it all later!'

He thrust the money into her hands and stormed out of the room, slamming the door with an angry and disgusted action that had her eyes filling with tears, and when she went back downstairs, they had already left.

For the next few hours, she went into every shop that the place possessed, buying two bikinis with matching wrap-over skirts, a beach robe and a bag, presents for Madeleine, Louis, Madame Benoir and everyone else she could think of. She was angry and hurt, determined to spend everything. But even after a splendid lunch out, she was still in possession of a great deal of money. She had been to the church, followed a suggested tourist walk pointed out to her by the man at the bureau, and although she was tired she did not return to the hotel until almost dinner time.

Gaetan pounced on her as she entered, jumping up from the lounge where he was sitting with Alain and Gabrielle and striding over to her as soon as he saw her.

'You have been on the beach!' he accused wrathfully.

'I have not!' she snapped back. 'I have been trying to spend your money but I'm afraid it wasn't possible. I'll keep it and have another go tomorrow. Money takes a long time to disappear when you have a sackful!'

'You look tired!' he insisted with an angry growl, and she faced him with a flare of temper that lit up her clear, grey eyes, angry herself that he spent so much time in correcting her and so little time looking into her heart.

'I am tired!' she burst out. 'After being shown the depths of my ingratitude I have spent the better part of the day walking round trying to off-load this bankroll!'

'I was angry,' he confessed, his eyes intent on her flushed and beautiful face. 'I offended you and I regret it.' When she simply stared at him with wide and angry eyes he said in a placating tone, 'Come and take tea with us.'

'No, thank you!' Beth replied with tight dignity. 'I have had lunch, tea, coffee, ice-cream and chocolate. I have bought presents for people who will not want them and still I have a wad of notes! I'm going to rest and count the remaining money. Then, I'll make a list of the things that I owe you!'

'I have said that I am sorry,' he said stiffly. 'Do you wish to be called for dinner?'

'No!' she snapped, marching off. 'I'll be there!'

Her annoyance sustained her for the rest of the evening but it was no longer there when they sat on the beach the next day. Gaetan did not speak to her, and she was bitterly hurt that he spent every minute with Gabrielle. She had worn one of her bikinis, but after taking a look at Gabrielle's figure she felt thin and ungainly. Alain was all admiration, but Gaetan had hardly even glanced at her and he had stated that they would leave after lunch, about mid-afternoon.

She was glad now of Alain's company, and happy to agree when he said that he had tickets for a concert the next day in Paris.

'It is a charity show, a very dressed-up occasion,' he told her. 'If I pick you up at seven we can have dinner and then go on to the show. Would you like that?' When she agreed and showed a great deal of enthusiasm that she did not really feel, he asked quietly, 'Will you be allowed to come, though?'

'I can do exactly as I like!' Beth said flatly. 'Gaetan does not own me.' Alain looked at her deeply for a second and then smiled.

'Well, if you think it will be all right, is this a date?'

'It is!' Beth answered firmly, jumping up gladly when he suggested a walk along the beach. Anything to be beyond the range of Gabrielle's low and seductive voice. She was making the most of every minute with Gaetan, and the knife of jealousy was beginning to twist so hard inside Beth that she could scarcely bring herself to speak at all.

Alain took her hand and they splashed through the shallow water at the edge of the sea and later wandered in the rock pools that were close to the cliffs, but she hardly saw anything that he pointed out to her; her mind was given almost totally to her own misery and to Gaetan.

Alain was intent upon making her happy, she knew. It was not possible fully to hide the distress in her eyes, even though she smiled until her face was strained with the effort.

'Let's get right away from those two,' Alain suggested. 'They are beginning to get on my nerves. There is another little cove around here.'

He began to climb the shallow steps cut into the cliff face and Beth followed dejectedly, only half listening to his voice, the sound of the sea a sad and lonely music in her ears. It was therefore not until she was some way up that the reality of her position dawned on her. Once again she had wandered into danger and the familiar tightness, the familiar dizziness began to grip her as she looked down and saw that she was half-way up the cliff, rocks below her, the sea, grey and calm, a backdrop to her situation. One second more and she knew she would freeze, would sway and fall to the rocks below. They were not too far up but the drop was dangerous, and compelling to her terrified mind.

'Gaetan!' She had screamed his name before she could begin to think that Alain was closer and though she did not now see him, he reacted with a speed that left Alain standing a few feet above her as if he were frozen into immobility.

Like a tiger Gaetan took the cliff steps two at a time and before she could fall his arms were tightly round her, his voice soothing and calming in her ear as he lifted her against him.

'It's all right, all right,' he murmured coaxingly. 'Just relax, *petite*, and we will soon be on the sand. Come along.'

Carefully balanced, he went back down the steps, his burden clasped tightly to him, and even when he reached the soft sand he held her closely, not putting her down.

Naturally Gabrielle had followed when Gaetan had taken off at such a speed at the sound of Beth's voice and now she stood looking at them both, her face for once showing nothing but surprise. She was no more surprised than Alain.

'What happened?' He had followed them down the steps and now he stood beside them, his eyes on Beth's pale face, Gaetan's grim expression making him realise that there was something here that was not normal.

'Beth has vertigo, severely,' Gaetan said quietly, his eyes on Beth's face as he held her against his chest, waiting for her breathing to return to normal.

'Well, I had no idea!' Alain protested. 'Why on earth did she . . .'

'She forgets sometimes, and if she is deep in thought or—preoccupied, she tends to walk into these situations. Now that you know you can watch out for it.'

'I can see that you know,' Alain said a little bitterly. 'She never told me.'

'Of course I know!' The words were wrenched from Gaetan's tight lips. 'I expect that she would have got around to telling you eventually, although it is not something that she likes to talk about very much.'

'So, she is afraid of heights?' Gabrielle murmured, her curiosity now satisfied and her annoyance asserting itself. 'Perhaps you had better put her down then, *chéri*. She is still not on firm ground.'

'I'm all right, Gaetan. Thank you for rescuing me.' Beth was not so far gone as she had been the day at the tower, and her misery was rapidly overcoming her fright. This was the last thing that should have happened. Now Gaetan would be even more annoyed with her and she had given Gabrielle the chance to use her waspish tongue with no way of stopping her.

'If you are sure,' Gaetan said in a tense voice. 'I think we had better go back to the hotel and pack in any case. You will not feel like lingering here.'

'That is a very good idea!' Gabrielle put in, her eyes narrowed as she noticed the way his hand still moved soothingly against Beth's arm. 'Personally I find the seaside a bore. It is all right for children but not for grown-ups.'

'I'm going to stay for a while,' Beth said quietly, not wishing to be with any of them at the moment, and Alain immediately offered to stay too, but Gaetan had other ideas.

'No, you can take Gabrielle back please, Alain. Beth takes a few minutes to recover.'

'You can all go!' Beth said in a voice that was sharper than she intended. 'I feel fine. I'll join you later.'

Gabrielle had already walked off to collect her things but Alain hesitated until Gaetan moved his head in the direction of Gabrielle with a clearly determined signal that told Alain he was to leave. Being alone with Gaetan was not what Beth had intended at all, and she dismissed him too in a firm voice.

'I'm quite all right, thank you, Gaetan. You can go too. I'll see you later.'

She turned and ran to the sea, plunging into the rather chilly water, wishing that there were somewhere else to run but realising that there was nowhere at all that she could ever go to escape from him. At least she would gain a few minutes alone now, and when they were gone she could come out and hide herself for a while. She swam out further and then after a minute turned back to the sand.

Gaetan was standing watching her angrily as she tossed the wet hair from her eyes, glad of the hot sunshine. There was no sign now of Gabrielle and Alain, in fact the whole beach was empty except for the tall and glowering form of Gaetan, his arms folded across his brown chest, his legs long and strong beneath the black shorts.

'I thought you had gone,' she said in as casual a voice as she could find, walking up the beach diagonally towards the towels in order to avoid him.

'Oh, no!' he bit out in a jeering voice. 'I really would like to be here when you kill yourself! I would not miss it for the world!'

'I can swim very well,' Beth managed through trembling lips. 'I've been swimming for years. I even have a small medal.'

'Do you also have one for stupidity?' he rasped in a caustic voice. 'I will have one prepared for you! You have suffered a shock sufficiently severe to chill your skin and then you plunge yourself into water that I would hesitate to enter without a wet-suit!'

'I'm fine,' Beth muttered as he strode up to her. She bent to pick up her towel but he snatched it from her and began to rub her arms and back with a great deal of angry vigour.

'You are not fine,' he snarled. 'You are simply crazy!'

'Let me go! I can manage without you very well!' She pulled the towel from him and turned her back but he spun her around, his eyes blazing with anger.

For a second or two they faced each other furiously and then all anger died from his face and he eased the towel from her and gently draped it around her, taking the ends and pulling her towards him.

'You make me very angry,' he muttered, his face darkening as he looked into her eyes. 'You walk into danger and nearly give me a heart attack and then you run away from me and plunge into an icy sea. What am I to do with you?'

'I didn't want you bothering about me,' she told him shakily and he smiled wryly with little humour.

'Bothering? What else can I be but bothered when you spend the morning on the beach looking like this?' He let the towel swing open, his eyes lingering on her slender hips and then on the swell of her breasts, his gaze narrowing when her breasts tightened beneath the searching eyes.

'You—you told me to buy it,' she whispered, horrified at the excitement that was even now racing through her, and he had not yet touched her, his hands were still on the towel.

'Sometimes I too am foolish,' he murmured. 'I never visualised how you would look in it, what little part of you there is in it.'

'Gabrielle wore a bikini,' she reminded him in desperation, but he only looked at her vaguely.

'Did she? I didn't notice,' he muttered. He let the towel go, watching its progress as it slipped to the sand, and then his hands reached out for her as if they were doing it against his will. 'It is ages since I kissed you,' he breathed, his lips searching her flushed cheeks, 'and I have never stopped thinking about it for even a second.'

As he drew her towards him her arms wound around his neck. If there was to be no other time than this then she would at least have this to remember and he accepted her instant surrender, tightening her to him, his breath leaving him in a shuddering sigh as he felt her skin against his, the length of her slender, silken legs smoothed against the hard power of his own.

'You never refuse me, do you?' he asked huskily, 'And I wonder why. Even when you were so very antagonistic when we were first in Paris you did not refuse me.'

She clung to him, her head tossed back, offering the slender length of her throat to his searching kisses. It's because I love you, she thought wildly, but that was something he would never know. Here and now they were as one and she would store this moment for the rest of her life.

'I should let you go,' he was whispering against her ear, his teeth nibbling at her ear with an almost painful intensity. 'I have no right to touch you, but in my mind I hear your little cries and I want to hear them again.'

He drew her to the warmth of the large bath-sheet that they had used to sunbathe and she snuggled against him softly and willingly, her arms clinging to him as he stroked her back. In her forbidden dreams she had been here in his arms before, her skin warm against his, his legs entangled with hers, his kisses burning her, and the reality was so much more erotic than her dreams, so much more overpowering. A small sound of longing escaped from deep in her throat and he gasped, turning her face to his, his hands urgent.

'Do you know what that does to me?' he demanded in a whisper, his eyes burning into hers. 'Do you know what your soft and eager body does to me? I am going out of my mind, and I cannot have you!'

A small whimper of sound signalled her distress, and her eyes were as grey as the sea, shimmering and pleading, and he groaned like a man in agony, crushing her against him.

'Open your mouth for me, *chérie*,' he gasped. 'Something must quell this raging fire!'

It did not, though. As her trembling lips opened he claimed them with a driving urgency that added flames to those already there and within seconds they were even more tightly together, drowning in each other, the sea a distant and unheard sound, the empty beach an island alone in time.

'Beth!'

He tore his mouth away to enjoy the pleasure of her smooth shoulders, his lips trailing hot kisses along their rounded softness and on to her neck. His hands were warm and hard, compelling her even closer, holding her to him as she struggled to melt into him and lose herself forever.

'I need to hold you, to touch you!' he murmured thickly. 'I have no right to touch you and yet—I must!'

His lips moved along the rising swell of her breast, his tongue flicking against the edge of her bikini-top as if tempting fate, a temptation that he resisted with a supreme effort of will, but he allowed his mouth to search for the hard peak and his lips covered it through the thin material, his teeth tightening gently on the hard bud and bringing a low moan from her lips.

'I want you, *tu comprends*?' he whispered hotly. 'I want to forget that you are anything other than a girl who is in my arms, eager to belong to me.' He raised his eyes that held their own torment. 'You do want to belong to me, do you not, *chérie*? At least, tell me that!'

'You know that I do!' she moaned. 'Love me, Gaetan!'

She pulled his head back to hers and for one lingering second, he tensed with passion, his hand sliding into the back of her bikini briefs, cupping her hip, his fingers flexing with desire, but with a low groan he released her and rolled away, leaving her trembling and bereft.

'No! I cannot! This is a madness and it must pass!'

'It won't! It won't pass, not for me!' Beth cried, tears in her eyes, her whole being aching.

'*Chérie!* It must!'

He stood and drew her to her feet, dressing her in her towelling wrap as she stood lifelessly with bent head. He wiped away her tears and drew her softly into his arms, cradling her head to him.

'Had it been anyone but you,' he confessed softly, 'I would not have resisted. I would have allowed myself to sink into heaven. But you are forbidden to me. The promise that I made to your uncle, the trust that I forced you to place in me that I am even now betraying, your whole life stretching before you, all these and more place you for ever beyond my reach.'

He cupped her face, forcing her to meet his dark eyes.
'Let us be honest with each other, Beth,' he said
seriously. 'Since we met, we have signalled to each
other in the ways of men and women since time began.
You did it even before you realised it, and I did it
even against my will. We have signalled with our eyes,
with our anger, with our laughter. We have had times
of gentle friendship, but always the air between us has
echoed with desire. Desire is not real, it does not last.
I have fallen into its trap before in my life and lived
to pay the price, to regret bitterly. I will not have you
with the same regrets. You have a future before you,
a whole life. I cannot offer you a matching innocence.' He bent his head and kissed her cheek ten-
derly. 'One day you will smile at this heated time and
you will realise that you were only just beginning to
be a woman and that I was captivated by you. We
will laugh at it together.'

There was a finality about his words that numbed
her and she shook her head slowly. It would never
pass for her. She loved him! His desire would pass,
though. Was she then expected to remain a friend and
see him with someone else who was more a part of
his world? Someone like Gabrielle? She rested her
head against his chest for one minute and then walked
off slowly up the beach, leaving Gaetan to collect their
things and follow.

Lunch was a silent and unhappy meal with both
Alain and Gabrielle in various stages of anger. It had
not escaped their notice that Gaetan and Beth had
been a long time in returning from the beach, and it
was not helped on the return trip when Gaetan's possessive voice insisted that Beth sit with him in the
front.

'I wish to keep an eye on her!' he said stiffly.

'I also have an eye!' Alain said with deep irony, not even blinking when Gaetan glared at him.

'My eyes know what to watch for!' Gaetan retorted, helping Beth into the front, and they were forced to comply with his wishes.

'Are you still coming to the concert tomorrow, Beth?' Alain asked as they dropped him at his home.

'Er—yes, of course. Seven for dinner and then the concert. We dress up splendidly, right?'

She smiled as brightly as she could but his annoyance was still thick in the air.

'I will call for you just before seven,' he said tersely, and his goodnights were stiff with anger.

Beth darted a glance at Gaetan as they drove off in the gathering dusk. 'You don't mind?' she asked softly.

'You will enjoy it,' he said evenly, no sign of any emotion in his deep voice. 'I would imagine that Alain is really good for you.'

There was nothing more to say. His desire seemed to have vanished as if it had never been, and she could hardly believe the words he had spoken to her on the beach. He was a man, and desire was nothing new to him. Love was new to her, though, and she felt the burden heavily, too heavily almost to breathe.

CHAPTER NINE

THE next morning, even before breakfast, he had gone, and Beth knew that this was the pattern of things to come. He would fight the feelings he had for her and would no doubt win; desire did not last, he had told her that. She could not fight her love, though, and she had no wish to. The only thing possible was to leave.

At lunch time when he arrived home unexpectedly she followed him into the library and brought up the subject on her mind at once.

'May I speak to you, Gaetan?'

He turned to her with a wary look on his face at the determined sound of her voice. 'Can it not wait? I am very busy!' There was a very harsh sound to his voice and she took a deep breath, meeting his frowning gaze firmly.

'No. I want to talk to you before you go back to the city.'

'Very well, Beth.' He motioned to a seat. 'We may as well be comfortable as we talk.'

'It won't take long. I'll stand, thank you,' she told him quietly and he shrugged, leaning against the desk and indicating by a movement of his hand that she should begin.

'I want to go back to London.' She said it in as even a voice as she could manage and he looked at her expressionlessly, clearly about to say nothing at all.

'I want to go as soon as possible,' she continued in a rush. 'I know that it will mean that you have to release a larger allowance to me, but I want to go.' Her voice rose a little when he simply stared at her and said nothing. 'Even if you won't release any allowance at all I...!'

'I will!' He went on steadily watching her. 'I will do anything you wish.'

She wanted to cry out and rush to him, begging to stay, but he turned abruptly and walked to the window, looking out into the sunlit garden, his hands thrust deep into his pockets.

'I will make arrangements for you. I have to be sure that you are going to live in a suitable place. By the end of next week, I can have everything arranged, I imagine, and then I will take you back.'

'No!' She bit back the frantic words that were on the end of her tongue. 'I prefer to go alone! I—I'm sorry...'

'Do not apologise,' he said quietly. 'I am accustomed to your decisions. I will make everything as easy for you as possible.' He turned to her and simply looked at her with dark and unfathomable eyes. 'If there is anything else?'

'No.' She clenched her hands, stopping them from reaching out to him, and his face was neither angry nor forgiving.

'Very well. I will arrange it. Now if you will excuse me, I have to go.' He picked up his briefcase and walked out and Beth sank to a chair. She had done the only thing possible, but it felt as if she had ended her own life.

She prepared in good time for her outing with Alain. She did not want him hanging around and finding out how things were between herself and Gaetan. Even so, he was there just a little too early and as she came downstairs he was in the hall with Gaetan.

'You look very beautiful, Beth,' Alain said with a smile of pleasure, and she took the compliment graciously.

'You did say that I must dress well for the occasion,' she reminded him, 'and this seemed to fit the bill, although I much prefer the one that I wore for my birthday party.'

It was out before she thought about it, and her eyes met Gaetan's with a kind of delayed shock. That night he had kissed her in the garden, awoken forbidden feelings, recognised her desire. Her face flushed and she saw an answering blaze of colour across his high cheekbones. Once again it was there, this aching, singing feeling that hung between them, and she moved towards Alain and escape.

'One moment!' Gaetan's voice stopped them and she turned to meet his harsh and unsmiling gaze. 'Come into the library. You are wearing a Vernais gown and we must make the most of it.'

He already had the safe open as she walked in followed by Alain and he turned to her with a glittering band of light in his hand.

'This will finish the effect, I think.'

He moved towards her and she stood trembling as his hands came to her skin, his fingers making her burn as he fastened the necklace around her slender neck.

He stepped back quickly as if he was making quite sure that the contact between them should be broken as quickly as possible.

'Good God!' Alain's voice was a shocked murmur. 'That thing is just about priceless! It's a family heirloom ... Hell! Gaetan, we'll need an armed guard with us!'

'It is perfect!' Gaetan said coldly, turning Beth to the mirror so that she could see the glitter of stones around her neck. 'It belonged to my grandmother, and that does not make it hundreds of years old. It is not priceless, merely valuable, and it is insured. I wish Beth to wear it!'

'All right, I'll take a cosh with me!' Alain said with little humour.

'It is up to Beth to accept the fact that she will wear it!' Gaetan said sharply.

'I—I'll take great care of it,' Beth said quietly, avoiding his eyes. 'Thank you for letting me wear it.'

'Do not allow it to spoil your evening,' he said in an off-hand voice, turning to lock the safe. 'Do not, either, let me keep you any longer.'

Her eyes met Alain's startled gaze and she was glad to get out of the house.

'What's the matter with Gaetan?' he asked as they drove off, and she managed a shrug of indifference.

'He's just annoyed,' she said vaguely. 'We don't always see eye to eye.' She knew that he was watching her closely but he said nothing further on the subject.

It was a successful evening and Alain as usual set out to charm her, and of course the music was beautiful, but through it all and even through the supper that they took later at a smart restaurant, Beth could not keep her mind from Gaetan, and her fingers strayed often to the glittering stones that he had placed around her neck.

She wasn't sure how she would be able to live without him. It was something that she would have to face because he would never change his mind, and he was not deeply involved with her anyway. Even if he had given her no encouragement at all, she would still have felt like this. From her first real sight of him, standing forbidding and alarming in the glaring light of her little room in England, she had felt a shivering panic that was not really fear. She had felt awareness.

As they drove back to the house she was silent, and Alain mistook her silence for apprehension.

'If you like, I'll come inside and face Gaetan with you,' he offered with a laugh. 'He looked very grim, and I would not like to see the very nice evening spoiled by a battle with Gaetan before you go to bed. We are very late, after all.'

'Gaetan will be either out, or asleep,' she assured him. 'There's only the hall light on, and I shall let myself in now and creep up to bed.'

'If you are sure.'

He suddenly leaned across and pulled her into his arms.

'Tonight, I will kiss you, Beth,' he said determinedly. 'I have been very careful and left you to show me that you want to be kissed, but I begin to think that I will be waiting for ever.'

She did not resist. Gaetan would never again kiss her and she was utterly without feelings as far as anyone else was concerned. As Alain's lips sought hers, she closed her eyes and accepted it, waiting for some of the explosion of feeling that she had when Gaetan touched her. Nothing happened at all except distaste that the lips were not Gaetan's and the arms that held her gently were not his.

Her expression showed her indifference and Alain's eyes narrowed on her icily cold face.

'You are not trying, *ma chère*,' he said softly. 'This time, you must co-operate!'

He lowered his head again but a wave of panic hit her and a feeling that she was in some way betraying Gaetan and her love for him.

She struggled wildly but he was too involved really to notice and his hand tightened on her neck, his fingers sinking into the softness of her shoulder, his mouth determinedly on hers.

'No!' She tore herself away, her frantic cry bringing him to his senses, and he released her, leaning back and lighting a cigarette as she strove to get her frightened heartbeats under control.

'Take it easy, Beth. You are quite safe,' he muttered angrily. 'You have always been safe with me. If you had not been, I can assure you that Gaetan would have allowed no outings whatever.'

'I—I'm sorry, Alain,' she whispered shakily. 'I should simply have said no at the beginning.'

'Do not trouble yourself, *ma chère*,' he said in a taut voice. 'I do recognise a refusal.' He paused for a moment and then said with an angry movement of his hands, 'It is Gaetan, is it not? You cannot bear to have other kisses!'

'Why—why are you saying things like that?' Beth pleaded in a distraught voice.

'Because I am, as you once told me, a grown man! I have known for some considerable time that Gaetan wants you very badly. It has not done much for my peace of mind either to see the way that you react to him! I know, however, that you are not entirely his possession, because there is a very hungry look about the pair of you that would not be there had you been spending the nights in his bed!'

'Oh! Please don't talk like that!' She put her hands over her ears but he turned on her and pulled them away.

'Why not?' he asked savagely. 'He has encouraged me to take you out when he knows that he has merely to snap his fingers and you will fall into his arms! My God! I will not forget the look in his eyes when the car broke down. If I had so much as laid a finger on you, he would have killed me! For one time-stopping moment, he thought that I had taken what he so desperately wants himself. Even Gabrielle has had little affection since he laid eyes on you; you have rocked a few lives, *ma chère*!'

'They can settle back to normal,' said Beth, taking a great shuddering sigh, realising that her friendship with Alain was over. 'I'm going home.'

'You are home!' Alain said scathingly. 'What other home is there that he will allow?'

'I'm going next week and I'm not coming back,' Beth said with unhappy finality.

'And he agrees?' Alain asked in astonishment.

'He is arranging it.' Tears welled up in her eyes, spilling on to her face, and Alain muttered angrily, throwing his cigarette through the open window and turning to hold her close.

'You love him,' he said deeply. 'I could kill him for causing you this misery!'

'It's not his fault,' Beth sighed, carefully pulling away from him.

'There speaks true love,' he mocked as he opened the door for her. 'I will not come in, Beth. I have no real wish to go for Gaetan's throat, and he would probably kill me anyway. It would not stop you from preferring the wrong man.'

She watched the car as it pulled away down the drive. She seemed to be at the centre of a growing circle of unhappiness, and her way of breaking it was all too clear. She should never have been here in the first place. She went inside and locked the door behind her, leaning against it wearily for a moment in the dim light of the hall.

'Back at last, I see!' the biting voice stated as Gaetan switched on the main lights and stood leaning against the library door, surveying her coldly.

'We had supper.' She took a deep breath and stepped forward, obliged to step into the brighter light now, and she stopped in growing surprise and fear at the look on his face as he straightened slowly, his eyes running over her, his face pale.

'And you finished off an enjoyable evening with a few wild moments in the car! Right here in front of the door!' His voice was wild with anger and he was white to the lips. 'I take it that you were once again seeking the excitement of a man's arms? I wonder what Alain thought of your wild little cries? Did they do to him what they do to me? Did he beg to hear them again and then lose his head?'

'He—he only kissed me goodnight,' Beth stammered, her hands shaking, afraid and unhappy at the fury in him.

'Just kissed you goodnight?' He was beside her in a few strides, taking her arm violently and dragging her into the library to hold her before the mirror. 'Look at yourself! You have been mauled like a slut!'

His words shook the whole of her body. She could see her bruised lips where Alain had forced her to accept his final kiss and she could see the marks of his fingers on her shoulders, but the contempt in Gaetan's voice brought her to full boil and she spun round on him with blazing grey eyes.

'Yes, I have been mauled! Not for the first time, if you remember! I have been really educated in France, thanks to you. Before I came here, I was simply lonely, but I had a life of sorts and I had friends. Now I have no one. You have taught me how to be alive, Gaetan, and you've confirmed my belief that the world is a cold and cruel place filled with

shame and hurt! You told me that I was clever. I'm
not. I'm really stupid, otherwise, I would have gone
long ago! But understand that I'll never be coming
back and I never want to hear of you again!'

'Beth!' He took a step towards her but she stepped
back out of reach, tearing at the catch of the necklace
and flinging it to the floor.

'Look at it! Cold, hard and meaningless, like you!'

She ran from the room and raced up the stairs, her
heavy skirts lifted to allow her to run from him, but
he had no intention of following. He picked up the
necklace that still held the warmth of her skin and
dropped it on the desk as if it burned him.

She sobbed on her bed for what seemed like hours
and then, wearily, she showered and put on her nightdress, her fingers plucking fretfully at the delicate lace
and silk. She had learned how to be a woman, how
to look like one, and now she would have given anything to have stayed as she was.

She slipped on her thick towelling robe and
fastened it round her, pacing the room. Now that her
anger and pain at Gaetan's words had lessened, she
recognised them for what they were, jealousy. Alain
had told her that it was obvious even to him that
Gaetan wanted her, and she knew that anyway.

He had lashed out with a burst of violence when
he had seen her and his tongue had been cruel, though
not nearly so cruel as hers. She could hear her own
words, so real at the time but now so cruel and hard.
She only remembered now his endless care for her,
the security he had wrapped around her, his constant
forgiveness. Her love for him forgave the stab of
jealousy even if it was merely from desire.

Her hard words had wiped out all that had been
between them, all that had gone before and she had

to set that right. She had to try. She opened her door and walked along to his room, hesitating outside, her courage failing her as she saw the light under his door. But she knew that, like her, he would not sleep easily after such an emotional upheaval and she knocked, her heart hammering frantically.

The door seemed to be torn open at her small and timid tap, and he stood looking down at her, his eyes hard and cold.

'You have thought of something else? Come in, *mademoiselle*! I would not like you to have to sleep on the idea. It is sure to be violent and painful as it is meant for me! Deliver it and then perhaps we can get some sleep!'

He stepped aside but she moved only a little way into the room, the harsh masculinity of it stopping her. There was not one item of clutter, not one soft colour. Expensive, modern and strictly functional, it was a harsh and lonely background for the man who now faced her.

'There is no need to shiver, *mademoiselle*,' he grated icily. 'I am prepared to take any further truths without resorting to violence. Say your piece and go!'

'I came to say that I'm sorry,' she said quietly, her head held up and her shimmering eyes on his face.

'There! You have said it and I accept your words at their face value. Goodnight!'

'You don't forgive, though, do you?' Beth asked softly.

'There is nothing to forgive. You have done what good breeding dictates. You have offered your apologies.' He turned away and stood with his back to her. 'We are now where we began many months ago, two well brought-up people keeping up the traditional face of civility. That is what separates us from the lower animals after all. The words you said before, however, came from the heart and the heart speaks only the truth.'

'I have not always been civilised,' Beth said softly, 'and sometimes, the heart is too filled with grief to care much about the truth. I want you to know that when I've gone, I'll remember only the good things, the way we laughed together, the way you looked after me and how, for a while, I was happier than I've ever been before in my whole life.'

He turned back to look at her, his eyes shuttered and his face still, and she hurried on, not nearly so brave when he was looking at her.

'I think that, after tonight, I had better go at once. I really don't want to be here any more.' She turned away, feeling blindly for the door, but his voice, unutterably weary, stopped her.

'Very well. Louis can drive you to Calais in the morning. As you do not want to wait, I cannot make arrangements for your living accommodation, but I will see that you have plenty of money. I will send your things on or you can take them. I promise that you will be away from here tomorrow if that is what you wish.'

'There's nothing else to wish for.' She sighed shakily and moved to pull the door open.

'You are doing what you want! What you have decided!' he said tiredly. 'Whatever else you wish, tell me and I will see to it that your wishes are granted.'

'Oh, no!' She turned as tears fell in streams down her face, her laughter a little wild. 'My wishes can never be granted. You said that, Gaetan!'

'You are moving temptation away from both of us,' he said quietly. 'I bow to your superior judgement.'

'Do you? Do you, Gaetan?' she cried wildly. 'But then, it means so very little to you!' She turned blindly away but his voice stopped her.

'You know that is not true!' There was an aggressive intensity in his voice that kept her pinned to the spot. 'Tonight—I wanted to kill Alain for even thinking of touching you!'

'Then don't send me away,' she whispered, her head resting against the hard comfort of the door.

'*Dieu!* You are going of your own free will. I am not sending you. I do not have that kind of courage! You are leaving because it is what you want!'

'I want you!' she wept. 'Nothing more.'

His hands grasped her shoulders, almost crushingly, his voice desperate.

'You don't know what you are saying! It will ruin your life! You have your whole future before you, a whole world to see. I want only what is best for you, I . . .' His voice faded as she simply stood and looked up at him, her heart in her eyes, his words rolling over her with no effect. 'If I hold you, I will never let you go,' he murmured, his fingers coming to trace the glitter of tears on her face with a kind of wonder. 'I have put you from me twice and I cannot do it again ever. You are crying for me and—I need you so badly!'

She moved into his arms, leaving him no time to protest, and he crushed her to him, murmuring her name as she wound her arms around his waist and clung to him as if she would never let go, her breath a sigh of contentment as his hand came to caress her hair.

'I feel like the devil who has tempted an angel,' he said unevenly. 'Now, I am almost afraid of my victory, but I know what I have known for a very long time, I cannot let anyone else have you.'

She lifted her face, still wet with tears, and he looked down at her with a smile in his eyes.

'Do not cry, *mon amie*,' he said deeply. 'I will not let you go.' The sensuous lips curved into a smile and

his eyes began to blaze into hers. *'Tu es si belle, mon
ange,'* he murmured against her lips. 'I want every
part of you and though I am the devil himself, tonight I will make you happy.'

His arms enveloped her completely, crushing her
slender body to his, a shudder of triumph racing
through him at her complete and instant surrender.
She felt it race through his body, a body that hardened
against hers immediately, signalling his waiting need,
and her soft lips opened beneath his driving demand,
no fear in her at all as his hands closed possessively
around the silken softness of her body.

'You are not afraid?' he muttered thickly against
her mouth and she shook her head, words utterly
beyond her, her heart racing beneath his hand as he
pushed the thick robe away and covered the pounding
rhythm with his palm, his fingers brushing the rise of
her breast.

'Let me look at you, *chérie*!' He slid away the thin
straps of her nightdress, allowing it to glide from her
slender body to the floor, and her face blazed with
colour at the flare of passion in his eyes.

'No,' he said softly as she crossed her arms over
her breasts. 'Do not be shy with me. You are beautiful.' He drew her hands away. *'Viens, chérie.'* He
guided her hands to his chest, urging her to remove
the white shirt that was open now to the waist, and
her eyes followed the movements of her hands, her
breath small gasps in her throat as her fingers
lingered on his skin.

'You see?' he whispered, his hands covering hers,
pressing them to his chest. 'It is a need in both of us,
to touch each other, to look at each other, to find
each other beautiful and desirable.'

This time, she did not attempt to hide from the
glitter of his eyes. The way he looked at her made her

feel beautiful, and when his eyes at last returned to hers, she whimpered softly in her throat, reaching out to him as he moulded her to his hard body.

'I thought that I would never again in my life hear those small and eager sounds,' he said huskily, his hands restless on her slender flanks. 'I will make you cry for me, *chérie*, and I will please you.'

He lifted her and closed the door, moving over to his bed and placing her gently on the dark cover, his eyes devouring her as he undressed.

'Only desperation allows me to touch you,' he breathed, taking her in his arms. 'You are so perfect that it is a crime even to think of it.' His eyes roamed over her face and hair as his hand smoothed the golden strands from her face. 'I remember when you were a strange mermaid in this house,' he whispered, 'combing your long hair, your eyes calling to me like a siren, filling me with forbidden feelings, angering me.'

His lips trailed over her throat and down to the swell of her breasts, nuzzling hungrily against her until she twisted beneath him in frustration. 'I remember my shock when you came back that same day, a woman, smiling and secret, charming Alain and tempting me beyond reason. I wanted you then as I want you now, but I never thought that one night you would be here in my arms, crying out for me.'

He covered her mouth with his, all teasing and soothing past, only a throbbing urgency left in him, and the hands that held her now were sure and possessive. There was a heated madness in them both making him forget her innocence in his need to own her completely, and it was only when his kisses and stroking hands sent her spinning into a shadowy world where she threatened to leave him that he slowed the pace of their lovemaking, his hands cupping her beautiful and wild face.

'Gently, *chérie*,' he murmured against her lips. 'I want this to be magic for you. I do not want to hurt you.'

But she was too involved to have any fear, and she pulled him closer until she was impossible to resist, ready for him, in spite of her innocence, accepting the hard thrust of his body with a small cry of joy that matched the deep groan that shuddered through him.

'Ah, Beth! *Chérie!*' He clasped her convulsively and took her with him into an explosion of delight that ended only when their desperation came to a climax in a swirling release and she lay still and quiet beneath him.

For a second they lay and looked into each other's eyes and then his dark gaze roamed over her flushed face, his hand smoothed the damp hair from her forehead.

'Mon ange!' he said softly, his gaze intent on her. His lips stroked hers softly and then he moved to his side, taking her with him, enfolding her in gentle and protective arms and covering them both with the sheets.

'I'd better go,' she murmured after a while as they lay together in silence, but his arms tightened around her instantly with no chance of release.

'No! The night is not over and this night you stay with me. Tomorrow we will talk and look at things, but tonight I need you beside me while I come to terms with the fact that you belong to me.' He turned his head and captured her lips. 'You are mine, *chérie*, are you not?' he asked deeply, and she nodded, smiling into his eyes. It seemed to her that she had always belonged to him. There was nothing in life except Gaetan, nothing that she wanted.

In the morning she awoke slowly, unsure of her surroundings, everything unfamiliar. She looked around the room without moving her head and the fact that this was no dream brought a faint flush of colour to her skin. Painfully shy now in the light of day, she turned her head, looking for Gaetan, but he was not there, he was nowhere in the room, and she slid from the bed in a panic, finding her nightdress where he had dropped it the night before and getting into it hastily.

She was struggling with her robe, her face filled with bewilderment, when he came from the adjoining bathroom, his dark blue robe belted around him, his hands still busy towelling his black hair.

He stood quite still as he saw her, his eyes moving over her flushed and anxious face and resting on the nervous hands that struggled with her robe. He looked again into the eyes that would so clearly have liked to avoid his but would not allow themselves this cowardice, and he smiled slowly.

'You wish to shower here?' He indicated the bathroom, and when she shook her head, her colour deepening, he moved forward and took the robe from her nerveless fingers, fastening it around her as her eyes slid to the crumpled sheets. 'Hurry along then, *petite*,' he said quietly. 'Shower quickly and then come down to breakfast. There is a lot to do today and we have slept rather late.' He led her to the door and gave her a gentle push as she fled to her own room.

Trembling so much that everything was difficult, Beth showered and changed. She had no idea what he meant when he said that there was a lot to do today. Did this mean that she was still to go? In the morning

sunshine it was difficult to believe that she had been
so wanton and wild in his arms the night before. She
had given herself to Gaetan wildly, not once but many
times, and he had not even kissed her good morning.
Now that he was satisfied, was it all over? Was this
what happened when a man merely desired a woman?
She went downstairs, her face pale and her eyes
shadowed.

Gaetan was already there and after one look at her
he took her arm and led her to the library, closing the
door firmly behind them.

'*Alors!*' he said with what sounded to her very much
like irritation. 'It is clear from the look of you that
you are not about to eat until we have cleared the air.'

He frowned down at her pale face and she wondered how he could look so fresh and alive when he
had had so little sleep. The thought brought a fresh
wave of confusion to her face and he sighed deeply,
leading her resignedly to a chair then leaning against
the desk, his arms folded, his eyes keen and dark on
her face.

'Today, we have several things to do. I will take you
into Paris because we must choose a ring. Later, I will
take you to Madeleine's and arrange for you to stay
there for a while.'

'I don't understand! Why must I go to
Madeleine's?' Beth raised puzzled eyes to his and he
suddenly laughed, his eyes lighting up with mischief
as he strode across and pulled her to her feet.

'Your nerves are affecting me!' he said ruefully. 'I
will begin again. Until we are married...'

'Married?' Beth's eyes opened fully in a mixture of
shock and bewildered happiness. Surely he didn't
mean it?

'You do not wish to marry me?' he asked softly,
his eyes narrowing.

'Just because... There's no need...' she stammered and he grasped her face in a hard grip, silencing her.

'Unless you imagine that I will allow you to become my mistress on a permanent basis,' he rasped, 'then marriage is the next thing to consider! Unless you also imagine that after last night I will allow you to flee from me and return to London?'

Beth made a great effort and pulled free, turning away from him. She had been under no illusions when she had offered him her love and she did not want him to feel obliged to marry her now. He had been unhappy once.

'I—I wanted to...' she began uneasily, afraid to anger him. 'I have no desire to be a burden to you and you needn't feel obliged to marry me, Gaetan. I know that you've been married before and that you were unhappy...'

'So!' he said softly. 'My golden girl listens to gossip? You intend then to refuse to marry me for my own good? What then are your plans? To take up a place at Cambridge University—pregnant?'

She spun round with a deeply flushed face, her lips parted in shock, and he looked at her calmly.

'It takes only once, *chérie*, and if you will remember, it was certainly not once,' he said blandly. He pulled her towards him and folded her in his arms as he saw her shaken look. 'I thought that you wanted me enough to stay here for ever as my wife, but even if you do not, I will keep you. I asked if you were mine and I imagined that your eyes told me yes, and that your arms clung to me with a certain amount of joy.' He kissed her bright cheeks and whispered in her ear, 'You will marry me if I have to lock you up and feed you with a spoon for months until you agree. I am very ruthless about things that I want and I want *you*!'

He drew back his head and looked at her as she began to smile, her eyes meeting his happily, and he took a deep breath.

'Little minx!' he snapped. 'I am not at all sure how you will behave at any time.' He held her away from him and then relaxed into smiles. 'Now that another battle is over, perhaps we could eat and then we will get the ring. You will be engaged, my girl, before lunch time, and after that you will stay with Madeleine until we are married.'

'Oh! But I don't want...' she began frustratedly and he cupped her face in possessive hands, kissing her soundly.

'Neither do I,' he said thickly, 'but you are young and tender, a *jeune fille* still. From now on, we must behave decorously. It is good for the soul!'

CHAPTER TEN

MADELEINE was delighted and not altogether surprised. Beth suspected that she had already had some information from Madame Benoir, who had been told before they left the house, and she could now see the necessity for the move.

Once the news was fully out, there would be a great national and even international interest, because the world of fashion would be at great pains to observe and photograph her and also her wedding gown. There would be television coverage, news coverage, and within hours of the wedding there would be copies of the dress well on their way to being ready for the shops. The fashion world worked like this, and she was now a part of Gaetan's world.

The thought alarmed her and she sat abruptly as Madeleine explained all this. It was something that she would have to face, however, and she turned an anxious smile on Gaetan.

'It will be all right, *chérie*,' he assured her quietly. 'Nothing shall hurt you.' She smiled enchantingly at him. He had already dealt with another of her unspoken worries, that Alain would never be a friend again.

'It is little consolation, I know, Alain,' he had said as they had called at the warehouse after choosing a ring for Beth. 'You have lost the princess, but I would like you to design the gown.'

His generosity had quite silenced Beth, and Alain stared at him in astonishment.

'You realise what this will mean to me, Gaetan?'
he had asked. 'My name will be made overnight.'

'I know.' Gaetan had put his arm around Beth as
he smiled at Alain. 'Very soon, I imagine you will
have a rival establishment, and when the time comes
I will help all I can. In any case, I am superstitious.
I do not wish to see the dress until the wedding day.'

'And then, heaven help me if you are not delighted?' Alain asked with a sudden laugh.

'You have the general idea,' Gaetan smiled. 'Just
design a gown for my princess. You can have the
glory.'

Now Beth had a woman to talk to for the first time
in her life, and Madeleine was very pleased to talk;
it seemed to be her hobby. Every subject that Beth
mentioned was deeply discussed, and she now had no
worries about whether or not Gaetan still loved his
previous wife.

'It was because of this wife that Gaetan met your
uncle,' Madeleine told her one night as they sat up
late to talk.

'How?' Beth suddenly found herself anxious again.
'There was a great age difference. I've often
wondered.'

'Did you know that she died in a hotel fire?'
Madeleine asked and when Beth nodded she added,
'Well, had it not been for your Uncle John, Gaetan
would have died too.'

'Was he in the hotel?' Beth asked with a suddenly
pale face.

'No. He was going in to save her. John stopped
him, held him and finally knocked him out.'

'He must have loved her very much to...' Beth hung
her head and Madeleine sighed, putting her arm
around Beth's shoulders.

'I regret now having started this gossip session,' she murmured. 'No, he did not love her. She was a bitch of the first order. My husband had just died and Gaetan and I were very close at that time, each relying on the other I expect. Always, from the first, there were men and after just one week of marriage, Gaetan knew his mistake. It was not possible to catch her at it, though, until the night of the fire.

'Gaetan was here with me and we heard from a friend that she had been seen in the hotel with a man, an Italian as it turned out, although Gaetan cared not who it was. He set off to face them and to get rid of her once and for all, to free himself from the farce of a marriage, because although she had no time for him she could see that he was doing well and she was not about to give him up.

'When Gaetan arrived, the fire was already out of control. Guests were outside in their pyjamas, the fire brigade working, the police there and Gaetan tried to get into the building. It is one thing, Beth, to wish someone out of your life, but quite another thing to stand by and see them die. Your Uncle John was one of the guests outside, he too in his dressing-gown, and he stopped Gaetan's suicidal attempt at rescue. Finally he had to knock him out, and when Gaetan came round, even he could see that rescue was impossible. According to Gaetan, your uncle, in spite of his years, had a punch like a mule.

'We all became great friends, because afterwards Gaetan found him and thanked him. It grew from there and that was when we heard about his dear Beth, now our dear Beth.'

Beth suddenly found that she was crying openly, the floodgates of her unease opened, and Madeleine drew her close.

'What is it, *ma chère*? I have made you unhappy with my story? I thought that you would want to know.'

'I did want to know, Madeleine,' Beth wept. 'I love Gaetan so very much.'

'And he loves you,' Madeleine said with certainty in her voice. 'I have never seen such an expression on a man's face as when he looks at you. It is almost unbearable. I am not at all sure that it is even decent!'

'Oh, Madeleine!' Beth flung her arms around Gaetan's sister and they found that they were both in tears.

'That we are so stupid!' Madeleine said with irritation. 'We will have a drink and then we will discuss your trousseau!'

The days were a joy to Beth. She went around Paris with Madeleine, shopping and visiting friends. She spent time at famous salons as she gathered things that she would need for her honeymoon in Fiji, and there was never a moment to worry about anything.

In the evenings, Gaetan would arrive, impatient to see her, very discreet in the presence of Madeleine, but his eyes telling her how much this was taking out of him now that she was no longer there to fill his days and his nights.

Finally, the dress was ready and Gaetan drove her to the warehouse one morning so that Marie-Annette could give her a fitting. They met Alain in the courtyard and Gaetan remained there with him as they discussed some new alterations that they were planning for the building now that they had less pressure of work from the new collection.

Beth went upstairs alone to Marie-Annette and the final fitting of the gown and she met her as Marie-Annette was on her way down.

'Go up to the top, Beth. The gown is behind that partition, well covered from prying eyes. I'll be with you in a minute.'

Beth went up, walking to the back of the room and to the gown that she would wear when she married Gaetan. It was breathtaking! Yards of white wild silk flowing from a tight bodice, the long, smooth sleeves coming to a point at the wrists. It glittered with tiny pearls, and she could see what it would be like on the day. It was a dress for a princess, the princess that Gaetan had called her. Even if he did not love her as she loved him, he would make her happy and she would try so hard to make him love her.

A slight noise behind her alerted her to the fact that she was no longer alone and she swung round to see Gabrielle standing there, her face bitterly angry.

'So he has finally caught you and you are stupid enough to go through with this wedding?' Gabrielle said tightly.

'I know that you work here, Gabrielle, but this dress is secret. Only Marie-Annette and Alain are allowed to see it. I would be very pleased if you would leave!' Beth said, quietly angry herself.

'I have no wish to see the dress!' Gabrielle snapped as Beth flung the covers over it and stepped from behind the partition. 'I feel sorry for you. No dress will compensate for the sacrifice that you are making. I have begged Gaetan not to go through with this. Night after night while you have been with his sister we have been in his house and I have pleaded. It is unfair to you.'

'Do not bother to tell me that you have been staying at the house!' Beth said heatedly. 'Gaetan has been with me every evening and even if he had not...'

'I said night, not evening,' Gabrielle said with a smile. 'You do not deserve to be helped! Gaetan is

marrying you because he is in deep financial trouble.
You have seen how he throws his money about? He
has overstretched himself and the new salon in Madrid
was the very limit. In the end, he could not afford it.
You remember that he never even went, that he came
back to Paris? He is broke, my dear *mademoiselle*,
but as he has said to me, it is a merely temporary
embarrassment. You are heiress to thousands and I
expect that Gaetan will get most of it.'

'Gaetan loves me!' Beth advanced in a fury at this
wicked insinuation and Gabrielle smiled, walking away
as Beth followed.

'All you have to do is ask him,' she said tauntingly.
'He is down in the courtyard with Alain. He is not
prepared for an outright encounter, his face will give
him away.'

Beth stopped by the wall and stared at Gabrielle in
a kind of fascination. She had never seen such
wickedness on a face before. The woman was enraged
with jealousy and quite beside herself.

'Ask him!' Gabrielle flung open the loading-doors
and stood back pointing. 'He is down there! All you
have to do is shout down and ask!'

The doors had hit the outer wall with a reverber-
ating crash and Beth found herself looking at the sky
and into a space where there had been a solid door.
Below her was the cobbled yard, three storeys down
and her old fear rose in her throat.

Gaetan and Alain had looked up at the noise and
now he saw her as she stood at the edge of the drop.

'Beth!' Gaetan too seemed paralysed with fear. 'Oh,
God! This time I am too far away.'

She saw Alain take off at great speed racing for the
entrance to the building but she knew that he would
not get to her in time and so did Gaetan. His voice
was deep with dread.

'Beth! *Chérie!* This time, you must help yourself! I love you, *chérie*, and if you die, then I die too. I will never let you leave me!'

A great burst of joy leapt through her and she was no longer afraid, no more than any other person would have been. He stood looking at her as if seeing her for the last time, and there was no mistaking the look on his face.

She stepped back and aside, moving into the safety of the room, her legs trembling but her heart singing.

'Lean out and ask him!' Gabrielle hissed. 'You will soon find out!'

'I already know,' Beth said calmly. 'If you doubt that he loves me, lean out yourself or wait here until he comes for me!'

Gabrielle turned on her heel and stormed off just as Alain arrived breathless and pale to take one unbelieving look at Beth and then stride to the doors and clang them shut with violent force.

'Did she open them?' he demanded in a cold and vicious tone, and Beth nodded.

'Yes. It doesn't matter though, in fact, I'm very glad that she did. I think that I'm cured of both vertigo and stupidity, all in one fell swoop.' She smiled brilliantly into Alain's astonished face and then she fainted quietly and totally.

When she came round, Gaetan was holding her and she could hear Alain's outraged voice telling him about Gabrielle.

'It doesn't matter,' she heard herself saying shakily, 'I owe her a lot.'

'Not as much as I do!' Gaetan said grimly, crushing her into his arms. 'She is not on my staff from this moment!'

Beth could not argue with that. She felt that Gabrielle was quite dangerous and her jealousy would

stop at nothing, but for now, she was happier than
she had ever been in her life.

'I cannot understand why Beth is smiling after all
that!' Alain said wonderingly and Gaetan smiled into
her eyes.

'She is sometimes a little strange,' he told Alain,
not allowing his gaze to leave her face. 'But she usually
knows what she is doing and I am quite accustomed
to leaving her decisions to stew for a while. Sooner
or later, she gets around to my way of thinking.'

'You'd better take her home!' Alain said, no doubt
thinking that they were both a little mad.

'After the fitting!' Beth said determinedly, struggling to her feet and out of Gaetan's arms.

'You are not now up to it!' Alain remonstrated, but
Gaetan sat down and smiled across at her.

'Save your breath, Alain,' he said softly, his eyes
on Beth's determined face. 'It is impossible to move
her when she has made up her mind. I let things take
their course. I have to wait quite some time to get my
own way.'

His smiling eyes followed Beth as she walked off
behind the partition with Marie-Annette and Alain
suddenly grinned, his last worries about her dropping
away as he saw the love in Gaetan's face.

When they finally got to the car, Gaetan told her
that he had already been on the phone to Madeleine
while he had waited for her to have the fitting.

'I have told her that we are coming to collect your
things. You are moving back home!' he said fiercely.

'But you said...I remember that you said it
wouldn't be proper!'

'The hell with proper!' Gaetan burst out, starting
the car and moving off. 'We go home! First, we give
Madame Benoir your things and then we go out to
lunch. This afternoon, we curl up on the settee and

talk. Tonight we go to bed—together! I let you stay at Madeleine's for the good of our souls. My soul has had more than enough!'

Beth snuggled against him and he glanced down in time to see her secret smile.

'What now, minx?' he asked, his lips twitching in amusement.

'I never wanted to leave you in the first place,' she said softly. 'What will Madame Benoir think though?'

'She will be very pleased, I imagine. She has hinted that I am bad-tempered now that I am managing without you.'

'Are you?' Beth asked quietly.

'Yes, *chérie*,' he confessed. 'I find that I cannot manage without you. You will find that I am a very demanding husband. Does it worry you?'

'Nothing worries me, so long as you love me,' she whispered, and his arm coming tightly round her filled her with happiness.

It was much later as she lay in Gaetan's arms, his endless passion for her for the time being satisfied, that she told him about the way she had found that she was no longer afraid of heights.

'What did she say to you, Beth?' he asked quietly. 'You have not told me but I must know.'

'She said that you were with her here while I was staying at Madeleine's,' she said softly.

'And you believed her?' he asked, his hand turning her face to his.

'No. I know that you want me. I didn't believe her.'

He looked at her steadily. 'But there is something else, is there not?' She said nothing but he simply went on looking at her and she felt the need to tell him everything, facing it when she had to.

'She said that you were marrying me because I would soon be very rich,' she said quietly.

'And knowing this, you are still prepared to marry me, to be here with me now?' he asked quietly.

She would not even think of the implications of that. He had neither confirmed nor denied it. He had simply asked a question and his dark gaze was riveted on her face as he waited for her answer.

'Yes. I don't really care why you're marrying me so long as you love me. I don't care about money or anything else. I only want to be with you always.'

'Beth! My dearest Beth!' he said softly, crushing her to him. 'I am grateful to her for the chance to hear how much you love me.' He drew back and looked into her eyes with a light-hearted look that she had never seen before even when he was happy.

'Soon, you will have thousands,' he assured her, 'but money is difficult to get rid of as you pointed out to me, provided that you have enough of it. When you have little, it disappears, when you have too much, it sits there sullenly and grows.' He laughed into her startled face and kissed her deeply. 'I could not in a lifetime get rid of all my money, my sweetest Beth. You may keep your English pennies, I will not need them. I only want you!'

'She said that you came back without going to Madrid because you could not afford the new salon,' Beth told him, her face filled with happiness.

'I came back so soon because I found to my great astonishment that I could not bear to be away from you,' he said softly. 'I knew then that I loved you. I was furious to think that you had been out with Alain.'

'I hadn't!' Beth assured him, adding quietly, 'You never told me that you loved me until I nearly fell today. That's what made me get rid of my fear. I think it gave me a greater shock. I never realised that you

might love me. I knew that you—you wanted me but
I thought that you and Gabrielle . . .'

'Gabrielle was a part of my life before I met you,'
he confessed softly, 'but we have never been lovers,
if that is what is worrying you. I had thought that I
would never have any feelings again, would never trust
any woman with my life.' He stroked her face, his
eyes tender. 'My feelings for you were not even
reasonable. I was simply mad for you almost from
the first. Perhaps I should have said the words,' he
whispered against her cheek, 'but I imagined that you
must surely know. I cannot look at you with anything
but love in my eyes. I cannot bear it when you are
not there.' His hands moved over her with complete
ownership. 'I suppose that I have loved you from the
moment that our eyes first met, when I saw you
through that shop window in your strange attire with
your hair like a rope of gold down your back and
your beautiful nose twitching as you pulled a face at
that woman.'

Beth began to laugh delightedly and then suddenly
stopped as she remembered her life before she had
met Gaetan.

'If you had not found me . . .' she said softly.

'But I would have found you, my own,' he smiled.
'I was looking for you with the intention of giving
you a severe beating, but when I saw you, I could not
quite get my feet back on to the ground. They are still
not on the ground. I think that they never will be.'

'I thought that I was intruding into your life,' Beth
said, flinging her arms around his neck.

'And I feared that you would walk out of it,' he
whispered, tightening her to him and looking into her
upturned face. 'Do you know how much I love you,
my beloved darling?' he asked quietly.

She did. It was in his face, in his eyes, in the arms that held her close. She would never be alone again, and as his lips closed over hers, the unhappy past died away completely in the love that flowed between them.

Harlequin Superromance

Here are the longer, more involving stories you have been waiting for . . . Superromance.

Modern, believable novels of love, full of the complex joys and heartaches of real people.

Intriguing conflicts based on today's constantly changing life-styles.

Four new titles every month.
Available wherever paperbacks are sold.

Keepsake

Harlequin Books

You're never too young to enjoy romance. Harlequin for you . . . and Keepsake, young-adult romances destined to win hearts, for your daughter.

Pick one up today and start your daughter on her journey into the wonderful world of romance.

Two new titles to choose from each month.

ATTRACTIVE, SPACE SAVING BOOK RACK

Display your most prized novels on this handsome and sturdy book rack. The hand-rubbed walnut finish will blend into your library decor with quiet elegance, providing a practical organizer for your favorite hard-or softcovered books.

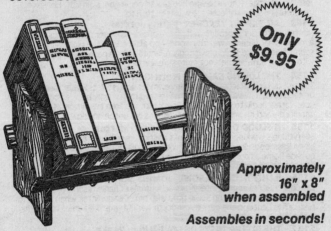

Only $9.95

Approximately 16" x 8" when assembled

Assembles in seconds!

To order, rush your name, address and zip code, along with a check or money order for $10.70* ($9.95 plus 75¢ postage and handling) payable to *Harlequin Reader Service*:

Harlequin Reader Service
Book Rack Offer
901 Fuhrmann Blvd.
P.O. Box 1396
Buffalo, NY 14269-1396

Offer not available in Canada.

BKR-1A

*New York and Iowa residents add appropriate sales tax.

Harlequin Presents

Coming Next Month

Available in March wherever paperback books are sold, or through Harlequin Reader Service:

In the U.S.
901 Fuhrmann Blvd.
P.O. Box 1397
Buffalo, N.Y. 14240-1397

In Canada
P.O. Box 603
Fort Erie, Ontario
L2A 5X3